Superhero Dad

by

Steve Moran

Also by Steve Moran:

Jackie Potatoes
Starallax Revenger
Barnabus Mudpatch

A Children's Book of Cats

Suzie Sparkle and the Magic Book
Suzie Sparkle and the Dragon Princess
Suzie Sparkle and the Bewitched Picture

Published by
Waxminster Children's Publishing
in 2015.
Cover by Steve Moran.
Text and cover copyright © Steve Moran 2015.
This book is copyright under
the Berne Convention.
No reproduction without permission.
All rights reserved.
The right of Steve Moran to be identified as the author of this work has been asserted by him in accordance with sections 77 and 78 of the Copyright, Design and Patents Act, 1988

**Dedicated to
Bonina and Raphael,
my own
Super-Heroes!**

Super-Hero Dad

Chapter 1

Accidental Accidents

It's not easy for me to say this because no-one ever believes me. They think I'm mad, or crazy, or just a plain old liar. So I've stopped telling people. In fact, you'll be the last person I ever tell because I'm sick of everyone's reaction.
So, here we go.
This is the truth.
Honest.
It's hard to say it, but...my dad is a ***SUPER-HERO!***
Please don't laugh!
It's true, I promise.
You're frowning.
You don't believe me, do you?
You're one of those people who always has to have an explanation for everything, aren't you?
And I thought I could trust you.
All right, then.
I can see I'll have to tell you the whole story.
Then you'll definitely believe me.
So, it goes like this.......

It was a dark and stormy night. I bet you've read that somewhere else before, but I'm not kidding you, it was. Thunder was rumbling, rain was pouring down, and there were flashes of lightning in the distance. It was darker than it should have been at this time of night, but dad always comes home from work in the dark anyway because he works so late at Kragell Industries.

But this night he was later than usual, and mum was getting worried. I mean, there had been so many disappearances lately. Mum hadn't wanted to move to Barnchester in the first place at all because it had a reputation for people disappearing, but dad said that we had to move here because of his job. There wasn't much work around for electrical engineers, you see, because of the recession, so he said he had to take whatever he could get, even if it meant working long hours every day in a town in the middle of nowhere that people disappeared from.

So it wasn't much of a surprise when he arrived home just as me and my sister Ellie were going to bed.

What was surprising, though, was that despite the rain, his clothes were burnt. Oh, and his hair was standing on end.

"Dad!" screamed Ellie. She was the first to see him come through the front door. I was the second but I didn't scream. I didn't say anything. My jaw just dropped.

I think it hit my knees.

You see, my dad never did anything out of the ordinary.

He did the same things in the same way every day, he wore the same kind of clothes all the time, and he always looked exactly the same whatever he was doing.

But now he was – well, totally different.

"Harry!" cried mum, and she rushed to help him as he staggered into the living room. He pulled off his smouldering coat, and let it fall onto the floor. "What happened?"

"Careful, honey," he said in a tired voice as he sank

down onto a chair. "Don't touch me." Some kind of green slime was dripping off him, and it was burning holes in the carpet.

He rested his elbows on the table and took off his glasses. You know, those round ones, like Harry Potter's? Well, he took them off and wiped his face with his sleeve. It didn't make much difference really, because both his face and his sleeve were covered in that green slimy stuff anyway.

He looked exhausted.

"Dad?" I said, tentatively. "Are you all right?"

I didn't really want to ask in case he wasn't, but I had to.

"What happened, dad?" butted in Ellie. She always went straight to the point.

"Don't worry. I'm fine," he said, wiping his face again. "At least, I think I am. And as for what happened – well, you won't believe me when I tell you, but I fell into a whole load of goo. All this green slimy stuff, I mean."

He shook his hand and drops of the green slimy stuff fell off it onto the floor. Where they landed little wisps of smoke rose from the carpet.

"How on earth did you do that?" asked mum, handing him a towel. He wiped his face on it, but that began to burn too, just like the carpet. Dad didn't seem to notice.

"It was an accident, I think," he continued. "I was in a part of the factory grounds where I'd never been before, and the rain was pouring down so I couldn't see where I was going, and I didn't notice that a manhole was open. The cover lay beside it. Someone had opened it for maintenance, I guess, and just left it like that. Well, I dropped through the manhole like an idiot and landed in this gooey stuff. It must have been a drain for all the waste products of the factory, because I think I've been dunked in a toxic mix of all the worst chemicals we produce!"

He smiled.

It seemed a weird thing for him to do, considering the circumstances. "Dad – why is that funny?" I asked. "You should be crying, not laughing!"

"You're right," he replied, "but that's not the worse thing that's happened to me tonight. The reason I was in a strange part of the factory was because I was being kidnapped by aliens!"

"Dad, be serious," admonished Ellie. "I think you're cracking up!"

"No, I'm quite sane. Or as close to it as I'll ever be, I suppose. But you see, I was leaving the office when a bright light shone down on me from somewhere above. I looked up and there was a flying saucer hovering in the sky, with the rain bouncing off it. The beam of light it was shining on me was something more than just that, because it began to lift me off the ground. I could feel a strange energy tingling all over my body, and the ship hovered above me, keeping quite still, while I slowly rose up towards it. Suddenly I believed all those stories I'd heard about people being abducted by aliens. It was happening to me!"

Mum let out a shriek. "I knew we should never have moved here! All those stories about people disappearing were true after all!" She started sobbing.

"Don't worry, Lucy," said dad, kindly. "You know I needed the job, and anyway, I'm perfectly fine."

After a few seconds he added, "I think," in such a

way that it was clear he wasn't.

I couldn't believe what I was hearing! My dad, my very own dad, had been sucked up into an alien spaceship! But then I had a thought. He hadn't actually said it yet. "Did it pull you inside?" I asked.

"Well, no," he replied, rubbing his eyes. "It was lucky that there was a storm tonight, because, you see, the alien ship was hit by lightning - and so was I! A double fork blasted down from the clouds and struck me and the ship at the same time. I fell to the ground and the ship disappeared!"

Mum started crying again. "Oh, my poor, dear Harry!" she said, "were you hurt?"

"Well, not by the lightning as far as I can tell, but I'm a bit bruised from hitting the ground. And in shock, literally. Which is why I didn't see the open manhole."

"Let me get this straight, dad," said Ellie. "You were zapped by some kind of alien ray that lifted you off the ground, then you were struck by lightning, and then you fell into a mix of toxic chemicals. That's awful! What could be worse than that?"

"Only one thing," said dad. "And that happened, too. You see, I didn't notice the alien ship until it attacked me because something happened in the office before that, something which left me feeling a bit woozy."

"Oh no, Harry," said mum, with tears in her eyes again. "So many terrible things in one day! What was it that happened in the office?"

Dad took off his glasses and wiped them with the smoking towel. It didn't make much difference.

"Well, I don't expect you to believe me," he said,

putting his glasses back on, "but I was bitten by a radio-active cockroach."

We didn't say anything. It was all too much to take in. But then I had to ask the obvious question. Well, someone had to do it!

"Uh, how do you know it was radio-active, dad?"

"Well, it came crawling out from under the door of the Isotope lab. You know, where they do all the radio-active research? It was making some funny fizzing and popping noises, which were most un-cockroach-like. Then it jumped onto my leg, and bit me through my trousers! I shook it off so that it fell onto the floor, and I was about to stamp on it when it exploded – in a tiny, mini-mushroom cloud! So I think I can safely say that it was radio-active."

Chapter 2

Garden Shower

We all sat there in silence for a few minutes, not knowing quite what to say.

I mean, I was shocked and amazed at the same time, and horrified too. A radio-active cockroach – yuck!!

The only sound was that of dad's slime dripping onto the carpet, and the soft hiss of the table, chair and carpet as the slime burnt holes in them.

It was mum who took the decisive action. Probably because we didn't have much money and so couldn't afford to replace the burnt furniture.

Mind you, it was usually mum who got things done in our house.

If only she'd got the super-powers instead of dad!

She would have saved the world ten times over by now, that's for sure.

And got everyone in the world to wipe their feet before going into their houses.

And brush their teeth properly.

And tidy up their rooms.

And do their homework on time…

On second thoughts, maybe it's better that she didn't get the super-powers.

She's bossy enough without them.

If she did have super-powers, she'd be super-bossy.

And that would probably be her super-hero name – Super Boss!

Anyway, some bossiness is OK, especially when it gets things done, like now.

Dad was making a mess of the living room like I

said, and he didn't seem to be noticing it at all, so mum took control.

She gave a final sniff, wiped her eyes, pulled herself together, and gave her orders. "Harry, go into the back garden. Now. Ed, you go with him and hose him down." (Oh yeah, that's my name. Ed or Eddie, whichever you like. Sorry I forgot to tell you, but it's been a bit hectic lately). "That's the only way we're going to get rid of all that gooey stuff. And do it quickly while I've still got some carpet to save."

Dad stood up without any argument. He was used to taking orders from mum, and I was too - of course - so I followed him through the kitchen and out of the back door into the garden. I could still hear mum ordering Ellie about. "Get a towel for dad and find him some old clothes. He's going to need them."

How mum knows these things I have no idea, but I suppose it could be her very own kind of super-power. Because she was dead right about dad needing some clothes, old or otherwise.

He stood in the middle of our small garden and held his arms out to both sides. Now that we were outside in the dark I could see that he was glowing softly. I don't know whether it was the gooey slime or whether it was just him, but he was definitely radiating a gentle light.

"Come on, Ed," he called out. "Wash it off me!"

Now it's not often I get the chance to squirt someone with a hosepipe. It's the kind of thing that usually gets me into trouble, especially if it's a grown-up I'm squirting. So it was with a burst of smug self-satisfaction that I grabbed hold of the hosepipe that we used for watering the garden, pointed it at dad and let him have it.

I hadn't meant to turn it on full blast but I guess I wasn't thinking straight. I mean, it's not every day your dad comes home covered in – well, you know the story.

So I hit dad with the maximum force our hose-pipe could muster!

And boy, was that powerful!

I mean, I already knew it was because I sometimes used it to shoot the neighbour's cat off the fence. I was only caught once, and I pretended it was an accident, but I have done it - well, let's say, a few times!

So I shouldn't really have been surprised when the super-mega-powerful jet of water hit dad and blasted all his clothes to smithereens, leaving him standing stark naked in the garden!

Well, I expect this wouldn't normally have happened to his clothes if they were blasted with a jet of cold water, but they'd been burned and corroded by the gooey slime, so I suppose they only needed a nudge to completely fall apart.

Which is what they did.

"Close your eyes, Eddie!" screeched dad as his clothes broke up into scorched rags and flew all over the garden.

I didn't need to be told twice. The last thing I wanted to see was my dad naked.

"But keep the hose pointed this way," he called out in a calmer voice. I was still pointing the jet of water in his direction, but I needed to be guided by the sound of him talking to make sure I didn't miss.

I could hear slapping noises as he rubbed himself down in what could only be described as a horizontal cold shower.

"I'm just doing my hair," he called out. "Hold it steady."

I wasn't going anywhere, so I did as I was told.

After a few more minutes of this, I heard a scream. It sounded like Ellie, who was bringing the towel and a change of clothes.

"Aaaaaaaaaaaaaah! Dad's got nothing on!"

"Don't look!" I heard mum say, so I guess Ellie didn't.

I certainly wasn't.

Looking, that is.

"Harry, what are you playing at?" said mum, sternly. "You'll frighten the children, and heaven only knows what the neighbours will think!"

"Sorry, dear," said dad quite cheerfully, not sounding sorry at all. In fact, he sounded quite pleased, as I expect I would have been if I'd just gotten rid of a load of slimy goo that was covering me. "You can put everything over there."

I don't know exactly where he was pointing, but I expect it was somewhere dry.

"Ed," he said to me, "keep it aimed this way. I'm turning round now so I can wash my back and my butt."

"Too much information, dad," I called out. The image his words had conjured up burned itself into my brain, and it was not a pleasant one, I can tell you.

There were more splashing noises as he moved around in the hose's jet stream, and added to them was the sound of him whistling.

Now this puzzled me. Why should he sound so happy and cheerful when he'd just had such awful

15

experiences?

"Are you OK, dad?" I asked.

The whistling went on for a few seconds more, as did the splashing noises, and at last he replied.

"I've never felt better in my whole life," he said.

Just then I felt a shower of water droplets. It was like being near a dog when it shook itself dry.

But dad wasn't near.

He was at the end of the garden.

"Dad," I asked curiously, "was that you?"

"Yep," he said, "I'm just drying my hair by giving my head a good old shake. Oh, and you can turn off the hose now. The goo has gone. But keep your eyes closed."

That went without saying.

I felt for the tap and turned off the water supply to the hose. It was still dripping when I hung it on its hook.

"Are you ready, dad?" I said. I didn't want to have to find my way back into the house with my eyes closed in case I tripped over something.

"Just toweling myself dry," he said, and then, after I'd listened to the sound of him putting his clothes on for a couple of minutes, he added, "OK, you can open your eyes now."

So I did.

And had a bit of a surprise.

There was dad, dressed in fresh clothes, looking as though he'd just come out of the shower with his hair still wet, but he seemed – well, different.

For one thing, he still had that glow.

It was only gentle, and if the garden hadn't been as dark as it was I wouldn't have noticed it, but he

16

definitely had a slight glow all of his own. So it wasn't the goo after all, it really was him.

And for another thing – he looked younger.

Not a lot, not enough to be noticed by someone who didn't know him well, but to someone who did, like me – well, he looked younger. Just a bit. Trust me, he did.

As if he'd had a really good night's sleep, or been on a relaxing holiday.

He looked refreshed.

Vital.

Energetic.

Full of beans.

Youthful, even.

These are not words I would normally use to describe my dad after a hard day's work at Kragell Industries.

And especially not after all the terrible accidents that had happened to him on his way home.

I mean, he'd looked a wreck when he first arrived, covered in goo. Now, he was like a different man, as though he'd gone through some kind of transformation, a transformation that had, uh, transformed him. Yeah, I know that sounds limp, but there you are. He was perkier, he was brighter, he was - all right, I admit it - not like his old self at all! Something must have happened to him to improve his mood by so much, and it could only be those accidents. Which was weird, if you think about it. But I had no more time to think about it because dad was dry, dressed and ready to move on.

"Come on, son," he said. "Let's go inside."

"What about the rest of your clothes?" I asked.

"The old ones, I mean."

We both turned and looked at the garden. The blast of the hose-pipe had torn the old clothes apart and scattered them in shreds all over the place. They must have been about to fall off anyway. They lay in little piles of rags, slowly smoking, and scorching the ground where they lay.

Dad surveyed the scene with equanimity. He didn't seem to be at all bothered by the sight of his ruined clothes. He'd especially liked the jumper that mum had given him for Christmas, but he was in such a good mood that he didn't seem to mind its destruction. That surprised me after all he'd been through, but hey, I was just glad he was OK. "We'll leave them there overnight," he said. "I'll clear up the mess in the morning."

It didn't matter to me when we did it, but I certainly didn't fancy picking up the gooey clothes while they were still capable of burning me.

"OK," I said, and that was that as I followed him into the house.

"Dad!" cried Ellie, and she rushed into his arms. "You're all right!"

"Of course I am," he said, returning her hug. "Why shouldn't I be?"

"Well, Harry, you did have all those accidents, didn't you?" It was mum, being horribly practical, as usual.

"I know Lucy, but I feel fine. In fact, I feel great! Much better than I normally do after a day at work!"

He let go of Ellie, and stretched out his arms. His T-shirt bulged. I'd never seen that happen before. Dad wasn't particularly known for his muscles – I mean, I can very nearly beat him at arm wrestling, and I'm not even a grown up. In fact, dad was more of a bookish kind of person. If anything, when looking at him the words "geek" or "nerd" usually came to mind. Well, normally, anyway. Before today, that is. I'd never – and I mean never – noticed anything resembling a muscle on him before.

But now his T-shirt looked tight on him, tight across the chest and shoulders, and tight on his upper arms too. For the first time in my life, he had biceps!

Something serious had happened to him, what with the glowing and the muscles, but he didn't seem to have realized it. I thought I'd better tell him what I'd discovered.

"Uh, dad," I said, just as mum was giving him a big kiss. She was obviously relieved to see him looking so well.

"Yes, son?"

"Dad, have you noticed that you're – well, that you're glowing? In the dark, I mean. You can't see it in the light."

"Are you sure?" asked mum.

"I am." I knew when I was right, and this was one of those rare times.

"Wow, I've got to see this," said Ellie. "It's so spooky! Let's turn out the lights."

We went into the living room. While dad and I had been outside in the garden, mum had cleaned it up. There were scorch marks on the carpet, on the table and on the chair that dad had been sitting on, but mum had got rid of the goo with old rags, so everything was safe to touch now.

Dad sat down on the sofa, and we all sat around

him. "So turn out the lights then," he said, and I did.

It should have been pitch black because there was no source of light in the room, and no street-lights outside the back of the house to shine in through the window either, for that matter.

But it wasn't pitch black.

Because dad was glowing.

It was only a gentle glow, but it was there.

And curiously, he flickered, like a candle.

And it shone through his clothes, through his jeans and his T-shirt.

"Wow!" said Ellie. "That's amazing!"

Mum was worried, though. She's like that. "Harry, I think you should go to the doctor. Or the hospital. You can't be well if you're glowing. It's not natural"

"I feel fine, honey, honestly," said dad. "And I don't think any illness they know about could explain this!"

"Dad?" I butted in, because I was beginning to think some very weird thoughts of my own.

"What is it, Eddie?" he replied, staring at his gently glowing hands.

"Dad, have you noticed anything else strange about yourself? Like extra muscles, or anything like that?"

"No son, not at all," he replied.

"OK, then," I said. It was time to test my theory. "Listen to me, dad. I'm just wondering if you might have changed in some other way too. I mean, all those accidents could have done anything to you, couldn't they?"

"I suppose so," said dad. "What are you getting at?"

"It's simple, really," I said. "I want you to imagine that even though you're sitting on the sofa, you're going to rise up into the air as far as the ceiling."

"Don't be ridiculous, Ed," said mum. "That's crazy. And your dad must be tired after a long day's work."

"No, it's OK, honey," said dad. "If Ed wants me to try it, I will."

So he closed his eyes and sat completely still.

All we could do was watch him in silence.

And then, without anything else moving or changing in any way whatsoever, dad floated up to the ceiling.

Chapter 3

Liking the Lecture

"I'm sorry, Ed" said dad, "but nothing's happened."
He still had his eyes closed.
I looked at mum.
She looked at Ellie.
Ellie looked at me.
We all looked at each other.
And then we looked at dad.
"Are you sure?" asked mum.
"Yes, of course," he replied.
"Then open your eyes," I said.
So he did.
And then he fell down onto the sofa with a crash.

"Dad," I said, in an exasperated way. How could he lose control so completely? "Why can you do something with your eyes closed, and then not do it with your eyes open? I mean, it doesn't make any sense!"

"Uh, sorry guys. I suppose I was surprised, that's all. I mean, when was the last time you opened your eyes and found yourself floating eight feet up in the air?"

I was a bit annoyed with dad. For an adult, he really could be quite dumb sometimes!

"Look dad, you're just not getting this, are you? Haven't you realized it yet – you've got super-powers!!! Anybody who reads comic-books could have told you that!"

Dad looked at me with a blank stare.
Mum and Ellie looked at me as though I was mad.
It was mum who broke the silence, and she did it

in that tone of voice she always uses when she tells me to tidy up my room or put my gym clothes in the washing machine. In other words, superior.

"Eddie, comic-books are just – just fantasy! They're not real! Harry, I told you we shouldn't have let him read so many!"

So many? What did she mean, so many?

I only had about five thousand comic-books in my room. DC, Marvel, Wildcorp, Printworx, Veemeister, you name it, I had it. They were all carefully sorted by title, number, age, category, style, colour scheme, sock size – well, you get the idea. I could find any specific issue you cared to mention – say, Z-Men number 743 – and I could locate it in under a second.

I don't like to admit it, because at school some kids laugh at me, but I am something of an expert on super-heroes.

And their super-powers.

And how they got them.

"Look, mum. And dad. Oh, and Ellie too, I suppose. If there's one thing I know about, it's comic-books. Not soccer, not pop music, not stamps, not cars, not TV shows, but comic-books. Trust me. What I don't know about super-heroes is not worth knowing, and the first thing every comic-book fan learns about is – origins. How did the hero get his powers?"

Ellie was looking at me with her mouth and eyes wide open. I wasn't surprised, really. I don't suppose I'd done much more than grunt in her direction for at least the last ten years. Well, she is my sister, after all. She'd certainly never heard me say so many polite words at once before, that's for sure.

I could see that mum didn't know what to think.

Her natural instinct was to shut me up, but even she was looking amazed. I suppose she'd never heard me speak so confidently before.

And as for dad – well, he looked pleased. I dunno, but I think he liked it when I took control. He was always telling me to be more assertive, to speak out in class and to stand up for myself against the bullies, and here I was, talking about something I really understood. To my family, the one bunch of people in the whole wide world who really ought to respect me.

And, much to my surprise – and for once in my life – it seemed as though they did!

"OK, son," said dad. His tone of voice surprised me. It was interested. Keen to hear more. Polite, even. "What do you think?"

I was flummoxed for a moment. My dad had never asked me that before. He was always so bound up in his own head, in his own job, in his own ideas, that I thought he'd never really noticed me – until now.

Oh, of course we played ball games together in the park, and board games at home on winter evenings, but he'd never treated me this way before.

Like an equal.

He'd never even asked me my opinion. About anything.

Maybe because most of the time I didn't have one. Or, at least, I didn't have one about the things that interested him – sport, politics, science, the news – so he'd never asked me before.

But now we were dealing with a subject that I really knew something about.

And I mean, really.

Super-heroes.

I took a deep breath and began my lecture.

"Look dad, you have just had a variety of experiences, any one of which has been known to give super-powers to the person having it."

I prepared my digits. This was where I did my ticking-off-on-the-fingers thing.

"Example One (and finger one). In 'Swamp Fiend' number one, Edric Clane falls into a swamp which is contaminated with toxic sludge from the nearby chemical factory. It turns him into a monster with enormous strength, psychic powers and invulnerability to toxins. Oh, and he glows in the dark." I raised my eyebrows and looked pointedly at dad. He nodded his head slightly.

"Example Two (and finger two). In 'Amazing Mysterious Legends' number 274, Farplin Bugler, an investigator of ancient curses, is struck by lightning while standing on top of a pyramid. This gives him control of electricity, the ability to fly, and the power to travel along electrical cables. His story continued in his own spin-off magazine, 'Lightning Man,' which is still running after more than 283 issues." I looked around the room. No-one spoke.

"Example Three (and finger three). In 'Secret Power Origins,' number eight, Dale Fargo, a jewel thief, is abducted by aliens. It turns out that the ray they used to suck him up into the space-ship gave him the ability to see through walls, make himself invisible, and communicate with ghosts. It wasn't the aliens' intention, you see, but it was an unexpected side-effect of the abduction ray on humans. His own magazine, 'Doctor Mysterious,' ran for 378 issues before he joined the Defenders of Freedomness, and his story continues there."

I paused for another breath. Dad was starting to look worried. I didn't blame him.

"And finally, the effects of being bitten by a radioactive insect are well documented. Think of Caterpillar Woman, who was bitten by a radioactive caterpillar, Slug Man, who was bitten by a radioactive slug, and need I say anything at all about the student who was bitten by a radioactive spider?"

Three heads slowly turned from side to side. We'd all seen those films together.

"So there you have it."

I was enjoying this. I wondered if teachers felt like this when they were in school. I wondered if there was a school for comic-books where I could teach!!! Plus, I'd never known mum or dad listen to me for such a long time at one go. And I wasn't even finished yet, either.

"Dad has experienced not one, not two, not three, but four events which are known to bestow super-powers. And while the kinds of super-powers these events can give are well documented in the comic-book literature, I don't believe there is any example whatsoever of these events being combined. In other words, dad may have extra powers no-one has ever had before because of the way these origin-events may interact with each other."

There was total silence for a few seconds. Then everyone started speaking at once.

"But what if..."

"Why does..."

"I don't believe..."

"Stop!" I cried, raising my hand. "One at a time please! You first," I said, pointing at mum.

She stood up, came over to me and put her hand on my forehead.

"Are you feeling all right, dear?" she said, in the voice she always uses when I'm ill. "I've never heard you talk like that before. For such a long time, I mean. Do you have a fever?"

"No, I don't!" I snapped, slapping away her hand. "I just know a lot about comic-books, that's all!"

Before anyone else could speak, Ellie butted in. "Eddie, that was brilliant!" she said, with wonder in her eyes. "You're so clever!"

I didn't know what to say. Ellie had never said anything complementary to me before. And I mean, never.

"You're right, Ellie, he is," said dad, speaking at last. The speech had been aimed at him, after all, so his was the response I was really waiting for. "He genuinely is clever. And I think he's hit the nail on the head. I can feel that totally different and peculiar things are happening inside me, and I have no idea what they are. We can all see that I'm glowing and that I can float up to the ceiling, but what else I can do is anyone's guess.

"So this is what I suggest. It's late, and we've all had an eventful evening – especially me! – so I think we should go to bed now. Even though tomorrow is Saturday and I still have to go to work, I propose that Eddie and me get up extra early and go and try to find out which of all those super-powers I've actually got. Is that OK with you, son?"

I couldn't believe the way dad was talking to me. I couldn't believe the way he looked at me.

With respect in his eyes.

He was treating me like an equal.

Like an adult.

"You bet," I replied. "Tomorrow we're gonna find out exactly what you can do. You and me. Together."

He stood up from the sofa, came over to me and held out his hand.

I took it and we shook.

"You and me," he said. "Tomorrow."

Chapter 4
Power Testing

The next morning me and dad got up early. And I mean *really* early, before mum and Ellie, and before anyone else in the world too!

And that's when it all began.

The legend of my dad, I mean.

Well, no, actually, it began when he had all those accidents.

So this was only the next bit.

Aw heck, you know what I mean.

So, like I said, me and dad got up early and set off for the woods. It wasn't cold, so we dressed lightly. I didn't want dad to destroy any more clothes, you see. Mum would have a fit if he did, and she'd destroy me too, even though it wouldn't be my fault. Probably. So I thought it best if dad didn't wear too many items of clothing. Just jeans, T-shirt and trainers. That's all.

Now I'd given this a lot of thought. Not that I'd had much time, of course, because we'd got up so early. But I'd been lying awake in bed for a long time last night, planning a whole program of tests for my dad.

We couldn't do this randomly. I needed to know what I was looking for, and how to look for it.

So I'd skimmed through a few piles of my comic-books before going to bed, and picked out some of my favourite heroes.

Then I went through the piles again, and picked out some of my less-favourite heroes.

I flicked through comic-books I hadn't read for years, some of them with really obscure super-heroes –

you know, people like Burger Master and the Space Fish.

With each of them I looked up their origins, and tried to find those who'd had accidents like my dad.

And there were lots of them.

Bitten by radioactive insects, struck by lightning, zapped by alien rays, dunked in chemical goo – there were zillions of super-heroes whose super-hero life had begun with accidents like these!

And as for their powers!

There were lots!

And I really mean *lots*!

So I began to build up a mental file of powers that dad might have, and started assessing the probability of him having them.

Flying?

Almost certainly. He could float, couldn't he?

Super strength? Pretty likely too. Insects were usually stronger than they seemed, and toxic chemical goo was always a good one for enhancing the muscles.

It was all getting a bit too much for me to remember, so I took out a notebook – I had lots of school ones with nothing written in them! – and listed possible powers, grading them from least likely to most likely.

Then I had to think about how we would test for each of them, and measure their strength, on a scale of, say, one to ten.

And then there were the great unknowns. I mean, any respectable super-hero just had one origin event that gave him his powers, but my dad had four!

Heaven only knows how they would interact inside him.

They might even cancel each other out!

That was a worrying thought.

Anyway, I made a list of all the powers I could think of, leaving space for a few more that hadn't occurred to me yet.

Then I drifted off to sleep, dreaming of dad flying in the sky and lifting up buildings, but running through all my dreams was the niggling thought – why couldn't it have happened to me?

The morning was clear and dry as we headed off to the woods. It was so early that there was no traffic on the roads yet, so no-one saw us leave the street where we lived and head down across the field and into the trees.

I thought the woods would be a good place to test for dad's powers because we could easily get there without anyone seeing us, and because no-one would see what we were up to when we were in there.

You see, not many people went into the woods, not even dog-walkers. It was dark in there, and the trees were crowded closely together. They'd been left pretty much alone for a long, long time. No-one admitted it because they didn't like to appear soft, but it was pretty spooky in there.

So spooky, in fact, that you didn't even get teenagers making dens, or lighting fires, or sneaking there in the evenings to get away from their parents.

No, and I could understand why.

It was truly creepy.

But funnily enough, I liked it. I always had. To me, it wasn't a spooky place at all, it was a magical one. A place where I could go and hide from everyday people and events.

A timeless place with no past and no future.
Only now.
An eternal present.
And a place where I could read.
When I didn't want anyone to know where I was, or what I was reading.
Like comic-books.
So it wasn't surprising that I should choose this location to test dad's powers.
It was a magical place, and dad had become a magical being.
Well, to me, anyway.
And – who knows? – one day to the rest of the world as well.

Right in the middle of the woods was a clearing. It was quite a large area, free of trees, with just a few rocks scattered around the place, rocks of different sizes.
This was my special place.
My own private, secret hideaway.
So it was obvious that I would bring dad here. It was so secluded.
The sun wasn't above the level of the tree-tops yet when we got there, so it was still gloomy as we entered the secret space.
Now the testing could begin!

"OK, son," said dad. "This is a good place to check for my powers – if I have any!" he added, jokingly.
I think he still didn't quite believe me, despite my speech of the night before.
Maybe he'd only come here to humour me.
Well, I would soon show him a thing or two!

"Of course you do!" I replied firmly. I didn't want him to start his new super-hero career with even a trace of doubt in his mind.

Everything we do in life is affected by how much confidence we have, so I wanted dad to have maximum confidence in himself so that his super-powers would be at their maximum too.

"OK, dad," I began, taking control of the situation. I'd thought about it enough, after all! Plus, I had to get things moving before he lost interest.

I pulled the checklist out of my pocket together with a well-chewed pencil.

"OK, dad, super strength. Let's see what you can do. Try this."

I pointed to a small rock. Well, I say small, but it was about half my size. It was only small for a super-hero.

Dad knelt down in front of the rock and studied it carefully. Then he frowned. "I don't want to hurt myself, Ed," he said. "You know, I've got to be careful. Mustn't strain my back and all that. Health and safety, you know. They teach us all about that at work. Let me check this out first."

He shuffled round the rock on his knees, examining it closely.

He didn't exactly look like a super-hero.

"It's too smooth, Ed," he concluded. "There's nowhere to grip it. How can I pick it up if I can't grab hold of it?" He looked at me as if I was supposed to solve his problem!

I was getting annoyed pretty quickly.

"Look, dad," I said, "you're a super-hero now! A rock like this is nothing to you! Just imagine it's a piece of polystyrene at work – you know, something light and flimsy they use in packaging to protect fragile things! You wouldn't think twice about picking up a piece of that stuff, would you?"

I was starting to doubt what kind of a super-hero my dad was going to be. He didn't seem very confident.

Why couldn't it have been me who'd had all those accidents?

I'd have made a brilliant super-hero!

Better than dad, anyway.

"No, I suppose not," he said, standing up and brushing the grass off his knees. He studied the rock carefully.

"Don't think so much, dad," I said. That was the advice Carpetmaster gave to the Creeping Terror just before he took over the world, and look what it did for him! "Just do it. Thunderman would have gotten nowhere if he'd spent as much time as you do just thinking about things."

Dad let out a sigh.

He really didn't think this was possible, but it looked as though he was going to give it a try anyway.

He put both hands on either side of the rock, and gripped it.

His fingers sank into the hard stone.

I let out a "Wooooo!" sound.

And he smiled.

Then, with no effort whatsoever, he lifted the rock up off the ground.

And threw it into the air.

He caught it with one hand, and easily held it above his head.

And he smiled again.

"I guess you're right, son," he said, tossing the rock from one hand to the other. "I can do it!"

"I knew it!" I cried triumphantly. "The comic-books do not lie!"

Chapter 5
Comics Dungeon

Well, we spent a couple of hours in the clearing in the middle of the woods.

No-one came near.

I knew they wouldn't.

They never do.

Which gave dad and me the privacy we needed for our experiments.

Or my experiments, actually.

And we found out that not only did dad have super-strength, but he could fly (although he wouldn't try flying higher than the tree-tops in case someone outside the woods saw him), he could send lightning bolts out from his hands, and project some kind of heat ray and cold ray too. Which meant he could burn things and freeze things whenever he wanted!

He'd be really handy at a barbecue.

Burning the meat and cooling the drinks!

He didn't think it was funny when I said that.

Well, he's pretty good at burning the meat anyway, even without his super-powers!!

He also had telekinetic ability, too. I mean, he could pick things up and move them around just by thinking about it.

Things like me!

"Put me down!" I yelled, when I found myself six feet off the ground.

He laughed when he did just that, a bit quicker than I would have liked!

He could run super-fast as well, of course, as fast as a bolt of lightning.

Plus he had the power to make his hair stand on end! If you can call that a power. What use that would be in an emergency I have no idea.

Oh, and he was still glowing. It was really faint, and nearly impossible to see in daylight, but if you knew what to look for - and I did - it was still there. I thought it was kind of cute rather than useful, but I decided not to say that to dad.

An unusual discovery came when he said to me, "anything else?" but without moving his lips.

"What?" I said. "What did you say?" I focused carefully on his mouth.

"I said – anything else?"

I heard it again, but his lips remained closed.

I gasped. I hadn't expected this.

"Telepathy!" I shouted. "Can you read minds?"

"I don't think so," replied his voice in my head. "But try replying to me just with your mind."

"You mean like this?" I thought, without actually saying anything with my mouth.

"That's right!" he sent back to me. "Now we can talk without talking!"

"Secret communication!" I blurted out. It was hard not to speak. I'd have to practice that. "Wow. I never expected this! It's just like Thinking Girl, but she was born with the ability. I didn't think it could be acquired."

"I think we're writing a new story here, son," said dad, this time with his real voice.

"Yeah," I said. "Cool."

And I meant it.

There had never been anyone like my dad before.

He was a new super-hero.

A new type of super-hero.

And I'm sure we hadn't discovered all of his powers yet, either.

"Hey, Eddie," he said, out loud again. "I've made another discovery."

I woke up from my daydream.

"Really? What is it?"

"I'm hungry!" he laughed. "Let's go home and have some breakfast."

"Good idea," I agreed.

I don't know how long we'd been out there, but it was a long time, and I was hungry too.

"Let's do it my way," he said, and I lifted off the ground. He didn't need to touch me. It was telekinesis again. He left the ground too, and we floated to the edge of the clearing where I banged into a tree.

"Oooof! I think you'd better put me down until you've had some more practice at this," I said, so he did.

He walked with me through the woods instead of flying. I expect he was worried about bashing into a tree himself as well - although I suspect the tree would come off worse!

We got home in no time at all, and then dad had to go to work. It was Saturday, but he always worked on Saturday. Sometimes Sunday, too. My mum said we needed the money. I didn't understand it, but there we are. And Kragell Industries - yeah, that really is what it's called; don't ask me why; I think it's German or something - well, they are a very demanding employer, and they expect dad to work nearly all the time.

It feels like that to me, anyway.

So off he went.

As soon as he was gone Ellie and mum were desperate to hear about what we'd been doing so early in the morning while they'd been asleep.

Dad had just eaten a piece of toast and drunk a cup of coffee and gone straight to work. He didn't like to be late - they were very strict at Kragell Industries - so he left me to tell them what had happened.

Over a bowl of cereal I told mum and Ellie what we'd found out about dad, and listed all of the super-powers we'd discovered so far.

Ellie couldn't listen quietly and kept interrupting with questions, and mum couldn't listen quietly and kept interrupting with suggestions for what we should have done.

But that's Ellie and mum.

Questions and orders.

I'm not sure how I managed to tell them anything at all, but I did.

And that was that.

Once breakfast – and the grilling session – was over, I needed time to think about dad's powers, and plan how we were going to test for some more of them, so I went up to my room, leaving mum and Ellie to their washing-up and their reality TV show respectively.

It was time to do some serious thinking.

I needed ideas.

I sat on my bed and began a thorough search of my comic-book collection. Not just a light skim like last night, but a real in-depth investigation. I kept the notebook and pencil nearby just in case I needed to record something, and started to systematically plough through the thousands of comic-books that filled my room.

First of all I trawled DC and Marvel, particularly looking out for different and obscure heroes.

Then I looked through the less well-known and less successful publishers. The second division of comic-book companies. Then the weird and the wonderful. The old and the out-of-date. The comic-books you've never heard of, and the ones you'd never want to hear of anyway.

I mean, I even had obscure publishers like Breggly Mags and Purnick Chronicles, and - lowest of the low - the rarely read and not very successful Zargexon Comics.

I kept all of the Zargexon publications – you know, like 'Kriozoc, World-Eater,' 'Earth Invaders,' 'Servants of Groaloz,' and so on – in my Comics Dungeon. It was a big cardboard box under my bed in which I kept all of the worst comic-books I owned, the ones I only collected because I was a collector – not because they were good, or worthwhile, or special, but because without them my collection wouldn't be complete.

I'd never met anyone else who'd owned or even read any Zargexon Comics except Dave, the King of Comics, who ran our local comic-book shop, Nineteenth Dimension. He was the one who'd put me onto them in the first place, because he knew I was an obsessive collector. And that was the only reason I bought them – because they were there.

I mean, their storylines were rubbish and the artwork was appalling, so there was no pleasure in reading and collecting Zargexons. It was more a sense of duty on my part, a feeling that there would be a hole in my collection if I didn't. So collect them I did, but I kept them in the Comics Dungeon so I wouldn't have to look at them unless I really had to!

Anyway, back to my dad and his brand new super-powers. I drew up lists and sub-lists of powers weird and wonderful – I mean, what about the ability to rotate your ears or to make your toenails grow? I hope dad didn't have either of those. And the ability to make chimneys stop smoking? I'm not even going to test for that!

Anyway, I was sitting on my bed surrounded by piles and piles of comic-books when – wham! My mind rang.

Well, it's like when the phone rings.

But inside your head.

Of course, it was my dad.

"Eddie?" I heard him say, just as if he was standing right next to me. "Can you hear me?"

"Dad?" I spoke out loud, and then realized he couldn't hear me speaking, so I thought the words instead. "Dad? Is that you?"

"Yes, son. I wasn't sure if you could pick me up so far away."

I could. It was as strong as strong could be.

"Yep, no problem," I thought. "You're loud and clear."

"Good. Eddie, I need to fill you in on what I'm discovering about my powers. And discovering with my powers, too!"

Wow. This was super cool. This was truly exciting! I'd been reading about fictional super-powers all morning and now I was about to hear about real ones from a real super-hero!

How amazing is that!

I focused my mind and gave dad my total attention.

"No-one's noticed you glowing, have they?" I asked. That would be really hard to explain.

"No, son, the lights are too bright in here. I can't even see it myself!"

That was a relief!

Suddenly a thought occurred to me. Maybe he was controlling it unconsciously! You know, turning it up and down as it was needed in dark or light conditions.

I made a mental note to check that out later. It was time to focus on dad's new discoveries.

"OK, pops. Go for it!"

It was weird to hear dad inside my head, but I knew I had to get used to it. This was the beginning of a whole new part of my life!

Dad started his story.

"Well," he began, "I went into the office as I usually do, but I found it really hard to concentrate on my job. Luckily, I'm working on my own today, programming a production line. I don't know what it makes, but I don't need to; I just follow the specifications. In fact, we never really know what we're doing, or what anyone else is doing either. Everything is secret, and we never work on the same project as each other at the same time. I don't even know what the factory makes!

"I say luckily because it's good no-one else saw what happened. I started typing the way I normally do, and broke the keyboard! I smashed it into tiny pieces! I didn't hit it, I just typed in my usual way, and I shattered it - with my fingers! I shuffled the bits into a bin and got a new keyboard, and then I adjusted my strength so that I tapped the keys as lightly as I could - and even then the keyboard bent!

"Anyway, there I was, trying not to smash things, when I realized the room was really noisy. Not just me being noisy, but…"

I knew what was coming. He was describing the experiences of Xeron Man almost word for word when he went to his office job after being exposed to the meteorite. "Don't tell me, dad," I butted in. "I already know. You've got super-hearing, haven't you?"

"That's amazing, son! How did you guess?"

"Ah, just genius! That, and a life-time spent reading comic-books!"

Chapter 6

Hear Here

"Well, I think you really are a genius, son! I don't know what I'd do if I didn't have you to help me with this!"

My chest swelled with pride.

And so did my head, too!

"It's nothing, dad," I replied. "Just think of it as the result of the years I've wasted by reading rubbish!" It was an accusation he'd often levelled at me when I'd spent a whole weekend immersed in my comic-book collection.

"Well, you won't hear me saying that again, I can tell you! You're my partner now, that's for sure!"

If I'd had a super-power which enabled me to glow like dad, I'd be doing it right now. He never gave me complements. For the first time in my life, he was starting to appreciate me!

But we had to move on.

"So what did you hear, dad?" I asked. It was hard to do this only in my mind. My mouth kept wanting to join in, but then dad wouldn't be able to hear me, and, what's worse, Ellie and mum would probably think I was madder than they already think I am if they heard me talking to myself.

"Well, it was weird," dad went on. "Once I'd stopped smashing the keyboard I realized that I could hear every little thing around me. The miniscule noise of the other guys typing was deafening. It sounded like a herd of galloping horses. Then their breathing started getting to me too. That sounded like the wind, and, what's worse, the real wind outside the window sounded like a hurricane!

"I could hear water in the pipes in the walls, mice squeaking under the floorboards, lots of creaky noises that buildings make all the time, and then - there was something else, something I couldn't identify, something that sounded wrong."

"What was it?" I asked.

"Well, listen to this."

"What do you mean, listen…"

"Be patient. I'm remembering the sound and sending it to you."

This was something new. I'd never even imagined a super-power like this before. And yet it was logical. If dad could send me his thoughts, then I suppose he could send me his memories too. What are memories if not thoughts? Just the same thing but different, I suppose.

I began to hear strange noises in my head. It sounded like a farmyard, or a zoo, but far away. There were growling sounds. And barking sounds. And guttural animal sounds, sounds of distress.

"That's weird, dad. What do you make of it?"

I was puzzled. These didn't sound like the kind of noises you'd expect to hear in a factory.

They were like noises from a zoo.

Or an animal prison.

Were people experimenting on animals somewhere nearby?

The thought was awful.

"I'm not sure," he replied. "They're so quiet that I think they're deep down underground, or at the other end of the site. But they don't sound as though they belong in a company like ours, an engineering sort of company that makes, uh, whatever it is we make."

As always, he was right. Did the noises come from Kragell Industries at all? Maybe his super-hearing had picked up something from a farm or a zoo or…I didn't know what else.

"Dad?" I asked. "Does anyone you're working with know you can do this? Are they looking at you strangely or anything like that?"

I waited a second or two for dad to look around.

"No," he replied. "They're both focused on their computers like I'm supposed to be. There's only Dave and Hank here, and they're wearing headphones. Sally is off today. These guys like to listen to music when they're working, so they're not paying any attention to me at all. In fact," he confirmed after a short pause, "Dave's on Facebook and Hank's on YouTube, so there's not much chance of them noticing any strange behaviour of mine, let alone doing any work!"

I detected a hint of anger during the last few words, because dad didn't like people messing about during work time. He was too serious to do that himself!

"OK, dad, are you allowed to walk around at work, or do you have to stay sitting down all the time?"

"No, it's fine, I can walk around. These two won't notice me anyway, that's for sure!"

"Then if you do that, as if you're looking for a book or something, then you could try and turn your super-hearing in different directions and see if you can locate that funny sound. It might be nothing, but it does seem weird."

"OK, I'll do that. I'll call you back when I've got something to report. Speak to you later."

My head suddenly felt empty. It's funny how dad

had treated our mental link as though it was a phone line, although I suppose it was pretty obvious that he would. It was like us both having cell phones inside our heads.

I decided to use this free time well, and do some more research. Dad was discovering new superpowers. He hadn't complained about everything sounding so loud until now, so it must have just kicked in. Could he switch it on and off at will, and had he accidentally switched it on, or were new powers switching themselves on over time, whenever they happened to be ready?

If that was so, I'd have to watch him carefully. It wouldn't be good if he gave himself away by accident. Also, if he suddenly developed an unexpected new power he might unintentionally hurt someone, or maybe even hurt himself!

I'd just have to be vigilant.

Meanwhile, I wondered what was the most likely thing he'd develop next...

I flicked through some old copies of "Superdude" and "V-Force," and the answer came to me. It was obvious, really,

"Dad?" I called out in my head. I was hoping this mental communication stuff really was like using a phone. If he could call me, then maybe I could call him.

No reply.

Well, in real life you have to shout to be heard from far away. Maybe it was like that with telepathy too.

I summoned up lots of mental strength.

"DAD!!!!" I shouted in my mind.

"All right!" he replied almost immediately. "No

need to shout!"

There was no point in arguing.

"What is it?"

"What are you doing now?" I asked, turning down the volume of my thoughts.

"I'm pretending to go to the toilet so I can listen around. The strange noises are either buried deep underground or are behind some pretty thick walls. So I'm trying to wander around the building and listen in different places without looking weird. I mean, I don't normally walk around these corridors. In fact, if anyone asks I'll pretend I've got lost while going to the toilet, but I doubt anyone will bother. Anyway..."

"Dad," I said, interrupting him. "Stop wasting so much time. I've got an idea. You could help your search by trying another super-power."

"What do you mean?"

"Well, you've got amazing hearing now, haven't you? And you didn't expect that, did you? Isn't there something similar you could try?"

"Well, I don't know, Eddie. I haven't read all of your comic-books, you know."

"You don't need to have done that, dad. We all sat and watched those Superdude films together, didn't we?"

"Yes, but..."

"So what did he use to find out what was happening inside the bank vault in Superdude VII?"

"You mean..."

"That's right!"

"Looking-through-wall-vision?"

"You got it, dad, although you could have given it a better name! So try and find out if you can look through walls."

I don't know about him, but that's something I'd love to be able to do!

Some people have all the luck!

Chapter 7
Underground Railway

I sat on my bed and waited for a message. I hoped that dad really did have looking-through-wall-vision, or X-ray-vision, or some kind of super-watching, whatever name you want to call it by. It should go well with his super-hearing, and would make him an even more impressive super-hero.

I wanted my dad to be the best, the strongest, the most talented and the most gifted super-hero the world had ever seen!!!

Although, of course, if he had this particular power it would mean that he would be able to watch me all the time, wherever I was, even when I was goofing off! He could check on me to see if I really was doing my homework, when I was actually re-classifying my comic-book collection or just plain old dozing.

We'd have to come to some kind of agreement.

Dad always kept his word. If I made him promise not to spy on me, then I knew he wouldn't do it.

I could always trust my dad!

Even if I wasn't so trustworthy myself!

I took a look at my watch.

This was taking longer than I'd thought.

I hoped nothing had happened to him.

"Hey dad?" I called.

Nothing.

"Dad?" I called again, a bit louder. I didn't really want to shock him like last time. "Are you OK?"

Nothing.

"DAD!!!" I screamed, if you can call a cry inside your head screaming.

"It's all right, son, don't worry," dad replied at last. "I'm just a bit confused, that's all."

"Phew, I thought something had happened to you for a minute!" I sighed with relief. "What's the news?"

"Well, it's complicated," he said. "Good, but complicated."

"What's that supposed to mean?" I asked, puzzled. "Can you see through walls or not?"

"Well, the good news is – yes, I can! The not-so-good news is that it's really hard to control. I mean, how do I know what to focus on? I can look through this wall, and the next, and the next, but it's hard knowing when to stop. This will need some practice."

Dad could be so annoying sometimes. I mean, he had no sense of urgency. If it was me who had...but it wasn't. I needed to give him some guidance.

"Dad, I understand it's new and confusing – I mean, it took the Sonic Twins years to get used to their powers – but you don't have years. Something weird is going on in your factory and you need to find out what it is right here and now! First you get attacked by aliens, then you develop super-powers, and now you hear strange noises with your mega-hearing. It's time for you to *see* what's going on too! You do understand that, don't you?"

"Yes, yes, son, of course I understand. It's just not always as easy as you think. These powers have hit me really fast, and it's hard to get used to them. It's not just a question of switching them on and off. It's more like learning a new skill, like cycling or swimming or juggling. It's quite difficult, really."

"Come on, dad, stop making excuses. Riding a bike is easy!" I was pretty good at it, anyway.

"Can you remember learning how to do it?"

"No, of course not. I've always been able to ride a bike."

"No, you haven't. When you were small you used to fall off all the time, even with stabilizers! It's just like that for me now. With these powers I keep – well, falling off! Now give me a few minutes while I play with this vision thingy."

Poor dad. He didn't even know the right words for his powers. What had he been doing all his life? Obviously not reading enough comic-books, that's for sure!

Seeing through objects was sometimes called X-ray vision, or super-vision, or super-sight, or farseeing eyes, or distance detection.

How hard could it be to control it?

I guess I was just jealous.

Why should dad have all the powers, and not me?

It didn't seem fair, somehow.

I'd been wishing for super-powers all my life and never got them, while he hadn't even given it a thought and got lots.

I knew all the right things, and he didn't.

He could do all the right things, and I couldn't.

Ah well, at least if we combined my brain with his powers, we should have at least one reasonably successful super-hero.

Anyway, I could communicate with him by telepathy. That was like having a super-power of my own, even if he was the one who was able to switch it on and off at will.

So how was the super-vision thingy coming along?

"Dad?" I called in my head. "What's the news?"

There were a few seconds of silence before he responded.

"This takes some getting used to, I can tell you," he said.

"Where are you now?" I asked. "Has anyone noticed you walking up and down and thought you looked suspicious?"

"Well, I had to get round that somehow. I had to find a place where I could sit uninterrupted and look though the walls without anyone noticing me. This is a big place and there are lots of walls."

I suddenly knew what he meant. I knew exactly where he was.

"You're sitting on the toilet, aren't you?"

"Obviously. Where else could I find solitude?"

There was no answer to that.

And anyway, the image of my dad sitting on the toilet and looking through the walls was not one I liked to dwell on. It didn't exactly say "super-hero" to me.

"OK, dad, too much information. Just tell me what you can see. Outside the toilet, I mean."

"OK, son. But this is not as easy as it sounds. It's all about focusing. And I'm trying to focus the hearing thingy and the vision thingy at the same time, and then combine them as well. It's not easy, but it's coming.

"I had to start with the office in the next room, and watch and listen to the people working there. And then move to the next room beyond that one. It means refocusing seeing and hearing together, but I'm slowly getting used to it. Beyond that is another office, then part of the factory, then another office, until I finally got to the car park and the road outside. I didn't find anything strange in the offices – just people doing their job."

This didn't seem right to me. I mean, there had to be something fishy going on. Dad just couldn't have been looking properly. I had to give him some sort of guidance.

"But dad, you said you'd heard some weird noises. Can't you find out where they're coming from with your super-hearing, and then use your super-vision to confirm their location?"

"It's not as easy as you think, son. But I'll try. I'm quite pleased I saw as far as the road, actually. But now I'm feeling a bit dizzy. Experimenting with my vision and my hearing both at the same time is quite disorientating, actually. I'm glad I'm sitting down."

I didn't want to dwell on the image that conjured up.

He went on. "Just give me a few minutes to recover, Ed. Then I'll explore further."

"OK, dad." I couldn't push him any harder than I had done already. It was amazing what he'd learned to do up to now anyway, less than twenty-four hours after the accidents. I mustn't let my own jealousy get in the way of helping him to discover and properly use his powers. How would I feel if I were him and he were me? I expect I'd appreciate some patience too.

He didn't take long to catch his breath.

"Right," he said at last. "I'm ready for another try. This time I'm going to listen as widely as I can, and not focus at all."

I wanted to keep dad as calm as possible. If he got stressed then we'd both lose out. "Cool," I said, as reassuringly as I could. "Just see what works."

I waited again which, surprisingly, was boring and tense at the same time. I just wanted dad to get on with it. I suppose it was easier for me. I wasn't having to make the decisions.

"Found it!" dad shouted. Now it was his turn to make me jump. I sat up straight on my bed and listened carefully. This was it. "It's coming from somewhere down below. Hang on while I try to find it with my eyes."

That was a strange way of saying it, but I knew what he meant.

"Well, well, well," he said after a moment. "It seems we have an underground railway station, right here underneath the factory, complete with a train! Amazing! I've never heard of that before!"

"Really? An underground train? Whatever for?"

"Well, it's being loaded up with pieces of metal. Shaped and cut pieces. Engines too, but I've never seen engines quite like that before. They must be made in a part of the factory I'm not familiar with."

"But what's happening to all this metal stuff?"

"I told you. It's being loaded onto a train."

"And where does the railway line go to? Come on, dad! Use your brains!"

"It's more of a job for my eyes, son! I'm following the track with my vision-thingy. Hmm, the tunnel goes on and on – it goes all the way to the Craggy Mountains!"

"But that's miles away, dad! Why would it do that?"

"Good question. I'll tell you in a minute. Ah, I've found the unloading place, and the metal parts are – Eddie, you're not going to believe this!"

He could be right. It had been an unbelievable day so far. "What is it?"

"People are using fork-lift trucks to transport the bits of metal from the train unloading-platform to an assembly area, where they're building – are you ready for this, Eddie?"

"As ready as I'll ever be!"

"Here it comes – they're building space-ships!"

Chapter 8

The Talkies

Space-ships!

Dad must be cracking up!

These super-powers of his must be melting his brain!

I mean, this was just a factory in Barnchester, after all.

But, come to think about it, he had been zapped by a ray from a space-ship, and the space-ship had to come from somewhere…

I had to find out more.

"Dad? Are you sure?"

"Yes, as sure as I can be when looking through walls and rock at an assembly line about five miles away under the Craggy Mountains. I'm damn well certain those things are space-ships!"

"What makes you think that?"

I wondered how he could be so sure.

"Well, first of all, they've got no wings. And second, they all look like the flying saucer thing that zapped me. Some are smaller, some are bigger, and some are the same size. It seems that this whole place has a single purpose – to build space-ships!"

"Look dad, I know I'm the one who likes sci-fi and reads comic-books, but even I think you sound ridiculous! I mean, an underground space-ship factory? It's not very likely, is it?"

"I suppose not, Eddie, but I can't help what I see, can I?"

"I wish I could see it too! It must be great to look

through walls and see a long way away!"

I had the feeling that dad was thinking. I don't know why, but because we were connected in the way we were I could sense that something was going on inside his head.

"Hmm, I wonder. If I can send you thoughts and sounds, I must be able to send you images as well."

"Come on, dad, even I know that's impossible. I've never ever read about a super-power like that. I mean, if…oh…"

I had to stop talking then.

I couldn't say a thing.

My mind had just been overwhelmed.

I was wrong about that super-power.

It could be done.

Dad was doing it.

He was sending me the images he could see.

His telepathy included not just sounds, but pictures too.

Moving pictures.

I couldn't believe it!

I closed my eyes to focus on what he was sending me, and my mind was full of what he could see.

Or, to put it another way, I was seeing through his eyes.

"Uh, dad?" I asked.

"Yes, son?"

"Uh, can you do that with the sound at the same time? I mean, I'm seeing through your eyes but I can't hear anything. It's like watching TV with the sound turned off."

"Let me see. This is a bit weird, you know. I can't believe I'm transmitting this stuff to you. I don't even really know how I'm doing it! OK, you want sound as well? Ah, let me try this!"

There was silence for a moment.

"Sorry, dad, no change," I said. I lay down on my bed and kept my eyes closed. I could see what my dad was seeing as if I was seeing it with my own eyes. I had to experiment with this.

So I opened my eyes.

And saw two things at once.

I could see my bedroom with my own eyes, and superimposed on it was the view of the underground spaceship factory as seen by my dad's eyes.

I began to feel dizzy, so I closed my eyes again and focused on dad's images.

The amazing thing was, I was sharing his super-power!

It was almost as if I was the super-hero!

As if!

"Eddie?" Dad spoke again inside my head.

"Yes, dad?"

"Can you hear anything yet?"

"Only you talking. Otherwise I'm still looking at the factory as if it was in a silent movie."

"OK. Let me try something else. Hang on!"

Then, I nearly jumped off my bed!

The silent movie had stopped being silent!

I could hear it now. I could hear the buzz and clank of the machinery, sounds that fitted with the images I was seeing.

"Dad!" I whispered in my head. "That's amazing! What did you do?"

"I don't know, Ed. What I'm doing is experimenting inside my head. It's just the same as if you had a new X-box. You press things and twist things and see what they can do. I'm only guessing, really. It's like having a new car or a new toy – I'm just playing with it. Can you hear what I can hear now?"

This was so weird that I was unable to reply.

I was lying on my bed in my room with my eyes closed, but I could see through my dad's eyes, hear through my dad's ears, and at the same time I could listen to his voice as he spoke to me.

"Dad?" I said.

"Yes, Ed."

"You know I'm right inside your head now, don't you? I mean, I'm seeing and hearing the same things as you – and I feel like I *am* you!"

"Well, I'm glad of it, son. I need a second opinion! This is all so confusing!"

I had to agree. We were two people inside one head. He was in control and I was just a passenger, but we were both sharing the same sensory data.

It was time to do something with it. "So what now, dad?"

"I was about to ask you the same question, son. I don't know, really."

It was all a bit weird.

I was sitting in my dad's head, and we were both sitting on the toilet.

This was not a scene you normally see in a superhero comic-book.

And it was time for me to take charge.

"Well, as I see it we have three options," I said, trying to sound business-like. This was despite the fact that I was bubbling with glee. I mean, I was inside the head of a super-hero! How amazing was that!

"One is; do nothing. Pretend we haven't discovered anything. You go back to work and I go back to reading my comic-books."

"That doesn't sound very exciting," said dad, "or honest either, especially as we seem to have discovered something quite disturbing."

"No," I agreed. "It doesn't. The second option is; we investigate more with your super-vision and super-hearing."

"Mmm, yes, that's possible. It seems a bit timid, though. And what's the third option?"

"That we go down there ourselves and find out what's going on. And kick some ass if we have to." I couldn't believe I was saying this to my dad, but someone had to tell him.

He didn't reply straight away. I didn't blame him. It was quite a decision, really.

Because what we should actually do - if you think about it seriously - is leave everything alone. Dad should go back to work as though none of this had ever happened, and I should just stay at home and have my normal lazy Saturday. Because if we poked around here we would run the risk of dad getting himself into trouble, and even losing his job. Who knows? We might possibly get ourselves hurt, or even killed.

But, on the other hand, dad had been zapped by a space-ship. And weird things had happened to him and given him super-powers. He'd already been affected by whatever was happening in that factory, whether it was overground or underground. Yes, he risked a lot by investigating further, but he'd already been affected by whatever was going on there – changed by it, in fact, into a super-hero!

I didn't know what he was going to choose, but I knew what I would have chosen in his place!

"OK, son," said dad's voice inside my head, "I've decided. Whatever's going on here has changed my life already, either for better or for worse. I don't really know which one of these it is yet, but I can't ignore it."

I braced myself for his decision.

"We're going down there," he said. "NOW!"

Chapter 9

A Distant Memory

Dad stood up and opened the toilet door. There was no-one about. Everyone was working.

"Dad?" I whispered in my head. I don't know why I whispered. No-one outside of dad's head could hear me even if I shouted, so that meant – uh, no-one. "What are you doing?"

"We're going to investigate, son."

This was so weird. Dad was walking through corridors until he came to a lift. It was all so bizarre. Because I could see through his eyes and hear through his ears while lying on my bed with my eyes closed, it was like being in a 3-D movie all of my own!

And I really was just a passenger in my dad's head. I couldn't hear what he was thinking to himself. I only heard him when he pointed his thoughts in my direction, when he intentionally shared them with me. It wasn't as though I was eavesdropping on him or interfering with his consciousness. I wasn't. I couldn't! I was just a hitch-hiker inside his thinking mind, seeing and hearing whatever he wanted me to.

And luckily, he knew his way round the factory – well, so far anyway.

We were in the lift now, and dad pressed the button to go down.

"Dad?" I whispered in my head again. I really didn't need to do it, I know, but I couldn't help it. "Dad? Where are we going?"

It really felt like "we."

I was aware of being in two bodies at the same

time.

One at home in my bedroom, lying on my bed, and the other standing in a lift, going down, down, down.

"We're going as deep as we can, son. The tunnel that goes out to the mountains is quite far underground, so we just have to keep going down until we access it."

I was starting to have doubts now, especially as I really was travelling with dad, inside his head. "Uh, dad, is this wise? I mean, if something weird is going on, then probably some weird people are behind it. And if it's all hidden under the mountains they probably don't want anyone to see it. So maybe you should just explore with your super-vision and super-hearing after all and report what you find to the police?"

"Nice idea, son, but who would believe me? No, I've got to find out what's going on for myself. And anyway, the space-ships I've seen are the same shape as the one that zapped me! Either they were trying to kidnap me or give me super-powers, and I doubt whether it was anything to do with turning me into a super-hero! No, I have to know who and what is behind this. I've been attacked and I need to know why!"

I'd never heard dad talk this way before! He was really annoyed. Agitated, even. Upset. It was hard to know which word to use! Sitting inside his head, as I was, I could feel a buzz of tension. He really was worked up about this!

Which is not normal for my dad. Usually he's very quiet, very calm, and wouldn't say boo to a goose, but this time he was tense. He was stressed. He was angry!

He was well and truly fuming!

And with super-powers like his, then I bet he could really do some damage if he lost his temper.

Suddenly, I had an idea.

"Dad? Would you excuse me for a few minutes? There's something I've got to do at home." I needed to look something up, and dad didn't need me on board right now anyway.

"OK, son," he replied. "Just stay connected. I'll call you when I find something."

"OK. Will do."

I opened my eyes at home, in my room, on my bed, and pulled my mind back from dad's head.

I sat up and tried to focus on the shelves full of comic-books in front of me.

I could still feel connected to dad, but now I was definitely back in my own body again.

Something we'd seen reminded me of - something else.

It was something I'd come across in one of my comic-books.

Something I'd noticed only today.

But I'd flicked through so many comic-books I couldn't remember exactly which one I'd seen it in.

I scanned the orderly shelves of magazines, carefully filed and categorized.

Which one was it in?

Which one of them was I trying to remember?

Then it came back to me.

The unlikeliest answer of all.

There was no mistaking it.

I'd seen a story about space-ships being assembled

in underground caves, caves underneath a range of mountains. Caves linked to a factory in a town by means of underground tunnels.

The artwork wasn't very good, and the comic-book wasn't commercially successful, but I remembered where I'd seen it.

It was in the Comics Dungeon.

In the rare oddity section.

The section full of comic-books no-one wanted, respected, or collected.

Except me.

It wasn't one of Marvel's.

It wasn't one of DC's.

It was a publication by Zargexon Comics.

Chapter 10
Flying with Dad

I jumped up and dived under my bed. Filed away in the cardboard box of the Comics Dungeon was my collection of the Zargexon Comics series, "Earth Invaders."

I picked up issue number 72 and flicked through it.

It all came back to me now.

This series was about how an alien race had conquered the Earth and enslaved humanity.

There were no super-heroes, no fighting back, only the total and utter subjugation of mankind.

No wonder it didn't sell well.

Who would want to buy a comic-book where the entire story consisted of nothing but doom and gloom?

Who, besides a comics nut?

Like me, for instance.

The storyline in number 72 rang a bell.

I turned back to page one and saw – dad's factory.

It had a different name – "Gringell Manufactures" – but it was obviously Kragell Industries to those who knew it.

It had been a long time since I'd read this series properly, if I'd read it at all. I mean, the artwork was so dire. It looked as if a twelve-year old had done it! A twelve-year old with dodgy vision as well – all the pictures looked watery somehow, as though they weren't quite in focus.

Marvel and DC had nothing to worry about.

I read the story as well as I could. The language

was awful. I'd always assumed it was originally a Japanese comic-book which had been translated into English by a Russian. Or possibly by an Eskimo. But anyway, by someone whose grasp of English was distinctly suspect.

All in all, it was a poor production.

But it was a comic-book which showed a factory like dad's, which was connected by underground tunnels to huge caves beneath a range of mountains where space-ships were being assembled by...

"Ed?"

It was dad, his voice sounding urgent.

"Ed? Are you still there?"

I lay down on the bed again, closed my eyes and focused on his voice. At once I was back inside his head, seeing what he saw and hearing what he could hear.

We were moving.

Fast.

It felt like being in a computer game.

"Dad? Are you flying?"

"Good. You are still there. Yep, I'm flying. I went down to the lowest level the lift could go to, and when I came out I used my super-vision thingy to find the tunnel. I punched through a wall to get there – I'm getting used to super-strength! – and here I am! I'm flying along it now. Can you see?"

I could, but not very well. It was fairly dark.

But hey, anyway, this was so cool!

We were flying in a long straight tunnel containing a set of railway tracks. There were dim lights all the way along it, which disappeared into the distance with the tunnel.

"And if you'd like to see more clearly you'll be happy to know I've discovered – this!"

Suddenly, as dad spoke, the tunnel filled with light.

"Dad," I exclaimed, "is that your glow?"

I couldn't believe it. He'd found a dimmer switch for his own radiance and turned the intensity right up.

"It sure is," he said proudly. "And I've found out how to turn it off as well, so I don't give myself away back in the real world."

"You did all that while I was back at home?" I asked. This was amazing! But then, my dad is a clever man.

"Yep," he said proudly. "I'm now a super-hero with my own built in lights!"

This was a good thing because it meant I could see quite far ahead now. But still, I couldn't help having a worrying thought.

"I hope we don't meet a train," I said nervously. I didn't think dad was ready for a fight with a locomotive – well, not yet, anyway.

"Sorry, son," he replied, "but we're about to. I can hear one coming!"

He was right.

I could hear it too, through his ears.

And there were moving lights in the distance.

Which were rapidly moving towards us!

I closed my eyes, forgetting that I wasn't actually there, but safe at home in my room. "Dad!" I cried out.

"Don't worry, son," he said quite calmly. "This is easy. I've been driving in Paris, remember?"

He was right.

Last year we'd been on holiday to France, and dad had driven us there. We drove through Paris, and my oh my, what a scary experience that had been! But dad had guided the car smoothly and safely through the swarms of traffic like a fish weaving in and out of a shoal of other fast-moving fish, each one of which was trying to overtake all the others.

Surely this would be much easier. All dad had to avoid was a train, and only one of those!

Which was now very near indeed, and heading straight towards us!

"Hold on tight, Eddie!" said dad, calmly.

It was a bit weird, really, because I wasn't actually there with him, but he was nevertheless behaving as if he was driving the car and I was a passenger in the back seat.

"Here we go!" he cried, and he flew as high up as he possibly could.

We were flying horizontally in the gap between the top of the train and the roof of the tunnel!

Where there was just enough room for one horizontal human being.

And that was my dad.

Flying at about 60 mph in one direction, while the train thundered even faster in the opposite direction.

In a matter of seconds it was gone.

"Phew!" I said, glad we were both still alive. "That was a close one!"

I had no idea what would happen to me if dad got himself killed while I was inside his head. It didn't bear thinking about.

But on the other hand, I wasn't sure he could get himself killed at all, anyway.

"No problems, son. Although mum won't be happy about my shirt."

He looked down, and I did so with him. There was a greasy smudge all over the front his shirt.

"Is that how close you were?" I said, not quite believing it.

"Yep. I just scraped it in a couple of places, but basically we were fine."

If I was dad I would have been shaking, but he seemed to be as calm as calm could be.

Maybe super-tough nerves came as part of the super-hero package.

"Good," I replied at last, pretending to be unimpressed. Back home on my bed I was quivering in terror, but here inside dad's head I had to remain calm, for his sake. "I'm glad everything's fine."

"Me too," he said. "But now we're in for some surprises. The tunnel's about to end, and I think there are huge caves beyond it. Any suggestions?"

"Well, we seem to have got this far unnoticed. Let's not spoil that, shall we? How about if you land and we creep carefully out of the tunnel and into the caves? Oh, and don't forget to turn off the lights!"

"Good plan. Let's do it."

Dad slowed down and landed on the railway tracks just before the tunnel ended. He switched off the glow and we were in near-darkness again. Then he hugged one of the walls and carefully peeped into the huge cave beyond.

"This is what I saw with my super-looking thingy when I was in the toilet, if you know what I mean," he said. "Or one of the things, anyway."

There were raised platforms for trains to unload huge pieces of metal onto, and fork-lift trucks to carry them away to other parts of the vast cave where workers were using the metal parts to build space-ships. Rows and rows of them, of all sizes.

"Look!" said dad. "That's what I saw! This is the space-ship factory! We've found it!"

The work was being done by men and women, but they looked dull and somehow suppressed. Their movements were slow and stiff, without energy or enthusiasm, and they wore grey uniforms so that they all looked exactly the same. I tried to remember if this matched the story-line in "Earth Invaders," but I couldn't remember, and I hadn't had time to get that far in the story a few moments ago. If there was a lull I could go back and check it out, but that didn't seem very likely at the moment.

"Something's happened to these people," said dad. "They're not normal. They've been turned into machines, or slaves, or zombies, or something like that."

Dad was right. There was no conversation, no chat, no joking going on. They showed no awareness of each other, and appeared to be looking at nothing except the task they were engaged in.

"Whoever or whatever runs this place has blanked out their minds," dad continued. "They don't look like the cause of whatever's going on down here, but they're certainly part of it."

"It's probably best if they don't see us, anyway."

"Agreed."

"Dad, how about scanning the area with your amplified senses? There's no point in us blundering around here randomly, is there? Who knows what we might bump into?"

"Right you are, son. I keep forgetting I'm..."

He didn't know what to say for a minute. Well, I'm not surprised. Neither did I, really.

"...I'm really quite powerful. Wait a sec." On the other side of the cave from the platform where the trains were unloaded was another gap in the thick stone wall. "I'm going to have a look in there."

Remember, I was inside dad's head. I could see what he saw, and hear what he heard.

And I could share his super-vision, too.

It was amazing!

I could still see the world around us – and so could he – but super-imposed on top of it was another image, like a film projection. The stone cave wall dad was looking at disappeared, and we could see what was on the other side of it. And what we saw there were machines flashing and humming, but as well as that there were other sounds, too.

"There!" cried dad. "That's what I heard earlier! It sounds like animals in distress – a cruel zoo or a bad farm!"

I could hear it too.

Growling and bleating and barking.

"Keep looking, dad. They can't be far away."

I could feel the pain in those noises.

We had to find the animals and free them.

Dad's senses expanded. He looked through the cave wall on the other side of the machine room.

And found them.

It was the weirdest, most shocking thing either of us had ever seen.

There were rows and rows of cages.

Cages with creatures chained to the floor, to the bars, to the walls.

But these weren't farm animals or zoo creatures.
No, they were something different.
There was only one possible name for them.
They were monsters.

Chapter 11

A Monstrous Discovery

Neither of us knew what to say.

So we said nothing.

And just stared.

There were rows and rows of cages, stretching as far as the eye could see.

And in all of them monsters were chained up, and they were distressed monsters, let me tell you!

It was the last thing I'd expected to see.

I mean, people in cages, possibly. Or animals, probably. But monsters? No way!

And who on earth had caged them up? It made no sense.

I was really wishing I'd paid more attention to "Earth Invaders." There must have been some clues in there!

"Dad? What do you make of it?" I whispered, even though no-one else could hear us.

"Well, I'm not sure yet. Look at their shapes." I did. "They're not native to Earth, are they?" I couldn't argue with that. "So we'd have to call them aliens, wouldn't we?"

"I suppose so."

"There appear to be two types. Green ones and brown ones."

"Yeah. Weird. Is it some kind of colour coding?"

"I don't know," replied dad. "And they're nothing like each other. The green ones are huge and bulky, like gorillas with claws and fangs. But the brown ones are completely different!"

"Yeah. They're more like some kind of gigantic bat

with claws and fangs. And they're hovering in their cages, without flapping their wings!"

"There could be some kind of anti-gravity field in there." Trust dad to think of a scientific explanation.

"I suppose so. But it looks as though they're designed for attacking things in the air, while the green ones are built for attacking things on the ground."

"Air troops and ground troops!"

"An invasion force!"

"Could be."

"We'd better tell someone."

"Hang on. Don't you think there's something suspicious here?" asked dad.

"Suspicious? No, not me. I mean, to have hundreds – maybe thousands! – of fierce-looking green and brown aliens chained up in a cave far below a mountain range seems perfectly normal to me. Don't you think so?"

"Ha ha. Very funny. Don't be sarcastic. You're not thinking properly, mister comic-book brain."

"OK. So, mister genius, what are you getting at?"

"Well, apart from the brightly coloured skin, what makes you think they're aliens?"

"Well, they're big, strong, ugly and fierce looking…"

"There's no doubt about that," interrupted dad. "But you're missing something. These creatures are basically humanoid in structure. Yes, they are big and ugly, but they have a strong resemblance to human beings, at least in a general sense. The green ones have two arms and two legs like you and me, while the brown ones have wings between – well, between two arms and two legs. Like humans have. So, you tell me, why would aliens from another planet have a basic structure resembling that of humans?"

"You're trying to tell me that they're not aliens, aren't you?" Dad always thought too hard. It was one of his more annoying habits.

"That's right," he said. "They're too human in their shape. The same body as you and me, only bigger, stronger, and, uh, a different colour. They're not aliens at all, but humans who've been mutated, either into muscle-bound freaks or flying bat-creatures!"

Dad was looking at them with his super-vision, so I was too. He was right. Someone – or something – was turning human beings into monsters.

Mutating them, as dad said.

I had an idea.

"What about those people we saw unloading the train and assembling the ships? They were human, weren't they? I mean, normal human?"

"As far as I could see, but they were curiously suppressed, as though someone was controlling them. I'm prepared to bet they've had their minds altered, while those poor people in the cages have had their bodies altered. Presumably the monsters aren't capable of doing the fine work of the un-mutated human hand, or brain, for that matter."

"So you mean that humans are being used as slaves to build space-ships, and they're being mutated into monsters as well, for – for who knows what?"

"Well, it doesn't seem very likely when you put it like that, does it? But I can't think of any other explanation."

"Dad! I've just thought of something! You know that people have been disappearing in and around

Barnchester? And I mean lots of people! Remember, it was all over the news? Mum was so worried she didn't even want us to move here because of it! You know how anxious she is whenever anyone goes out of the house? What if – what if these creatures are the disappeared people?"

"I think you're right, son. We've found the cause of the disappearances – but we still don't know who's behind it!"

"Well, now that we're here, we've got to find out! Can't you scan around some more with your super-duper eyes?"

"I can, but I'd rather get closer. I'm not so used to this super-duper stuff yet!"

"OK, let's go then. What's the best way to get there?"

"Flying, I suppose."

"Good idea. Dad, I was wondering about the cockroach that bit you. Do you have any insect-like powers? I mean, can you stick to walls and ceilings? Like you know who, the guy that was bitten by a spider?"

"I dunno. Let me try."

Dad looked down at his hand and so did I. He pressed it against the wall of the tunnel and then took it off again.

"Nothing," he said. "No stick at all."

I knew this couldn't be right. There had to be some advantage to having been bitten by a radio-active cockroach.

"Dad, you're not trying. When you put your hand on the wall you've got to *will* it to stick. It won't stick to anything unless you want it to, otherwise everything you touch would stick to you all the time, wouldn't it?"

"I suppose so…"

"So you have to *want* it. Try again."

Dad put his hand to the wall again. And this time it stuck.

In fact, when he tried to pull it off it wouldn't come away. It stayed stuck there.

"Help, Ed!" he cried. "It won't come off!"

"You have to *want* it, dad. You switch it on and off in your mind as you need to. That's what Centipede Man always says, anyway, and he has a hundred sticky feet to think about, so he should know."

Dad's hand pulled away from the wall.

Someone needed to take control, and, in the realm of super-powers, it obviously had to be me.

"So look, dad, we fly along the top of those cages, trying not to be seen. When you want to stop and look at something properly you use your hands to stick onto the roof of the cave. Just select the power you need for the task in hand. Simple, isn't it?"

I felt quite proud of myself, giving dad a lecture on how to use his powers.

"I suppose it is when you put it like that, son. I'll have to concentrate to do the sticking and releasing bit properly, but I think I can do it. Come on, let's go."

We crept out of the tunnel and looked around the enormous space-ship assembly chamber. Dad slowly floated up to the roof, which really was quite high. I didn't feel very comfortable, but he didn't seem to mind.

You see, I don't like heights.

Or, to put it another way, I *really* don't like heights.

But I told myself that dad's super-body probably couldn't be hurt if it fell down, even from here, while I was actually miles away, lying on my bed at home. Only my mind was here.

He slowly glided across the great chamber, hugging the roof. Sometimes he stopped and stuck to it with his hands. It gave us a chance to look around and get our bearings. And it gave dad the chance to practice sticking to things.

From so high up we could see all over the cavern.

It was really big.

There was the station area for the trains to be unloaded. And there were the fork-lift trucks which transported the bits of metal to different areas where they were joined together to make space-ships.

But this doesn't begin to tell you how big the cave actually was. It was big enough to have completed space-ships at the other end of it, rows and rows of them, vanishing into the distance.

It was an assembly line for a fleet of ships – could it be an invasion fleet? If only I could remember the story in that stupid comic-book! We had to find out what was going on as soon as possible!

We floated into the next cave, which I thought of as the engine room. It was full of busy humming and flashing machines with no-one in attendance, and then we left that to enter the cave beyond, the cave of the monsters. Well, that's the name I gave it, anyway.

We quietly slipped through the big gap in the stone wall, and floated up to the top of another enormous cave. From here we could see the rows and rows and rows of cages. The noise the creatures made was deafening.

Dad fixed himself to a central point in the ceiling so we could see everything, and we were just looking around to orientate ourselves when, without warning, everything went black...

Chapter 12

Eddie Alone

…and when I woke up I wasn't in my bed any longer.

I was in a brightly lit room, with a metal ceiling and metal walls. I was lying on something hard, like a metal table, and could feel metal bands around my wrists and ankles.

My head wasn't secured, though, so at least I could turn it and look around.

I was in a bare chamber with no-one in it but myself, with an enormous screen in the ceiling above my head, facing me, so that I could look directly at it. It was flickering.

It was only then that I realized that I *really* wasn't at home in my bedroom.

I *really* was here instead.

Wherever here was.

I twisted my head to look at my hands and arms and chest as best I could.

I was wearing dad's clothes.

And dad's body.

I *was* dad!

But where was he?

Something had knocked us both unconscious, and I'd woken up first, so now – the body was mine!

How weird was that? Before, I'd been a passenger in dad's head, but now I was the controller of his whole body. I could feel the metal bands on my wrists and ankles, I could feel the hard table I was lying on – and I could feel something else, something I'd never felt before, or even imagined.

It was a kind of energy, a kind of pulsing vitality, and it was quietly humming through my whole body.

This must be dad's super-powers!

It felt incredible!

It made me feel as though I could do anything!

I flexed my arms slightly, and felt the pull of the chains attached to the metal wrist bands. I knew that I could snap them easily!

But this wasn't the time to try – not yet.

Before I fought back, I needed to know something about my enemy.

About whoever or whatever it was that had knocked me and my dad unconscious.

Speaking of which...

"Dad?" I called out inside my head. "Dad? Are you there? Are you awake yet?"

No reply.

He must have been hurt by whatever it was that struck us.

Maybe he took a hit for me, which was why I was awake first.

I hope he's OK.

But I'll have to worry about that later.

When we're free.

When *I'm* free!

It was up to me to rescue his body!

But before I could do anything, the huge screen in the ceiling above me flickered into life, and a gigantic face appeared on it.

If so many weird things hadn't happened to me lately, I expect I would have been frightened.

Probably terrified.

But, to tell you the truth, everything had been so

weird since - how long ago was it? - only yesterday? – that nothing could faze me any more.

In fact, I loved it.

I was in a dream come true.

I was living in a story any comic-book would be proud of, and I was the super-hero!

I may be a prisoner, but I was a prisoner in paradise!

I reckoned I was prepared for anything.

Which was rather fortunate, because otherwise I would probably have fainted when the face appeared on the screen!

If you can call it a face!

There was something like a mouth in the middle of the – the lump, and several eye-like things were gathered randomly around it, stuck on the end of stalks. There were tufts of hair – or possibly very small tentacles – waving slowly around, and whether that was due to a wind or their own motion I couldn't say.

But anyway, the face was pretty ugly.

And I had a feeling I'd seen it before...

Surely it had been in "Earth Invaders" number 72? I wasn't certain, but I thought so...

That issue from Zargexon Comics kept coming to my mind, but I just couldn't remember enough about it. Anyway, I felt sure I'd seen this horrible ugly face in that comic-book first.

Which meant that any fear I might have felt was replaced with curiosity.

Why on Earth (or anywhere else, for that matter) was a monster from a very bad comic-book looking at me from a monitor in the ceiling of a prison in an underground cave?

I quickly ran through the possibilities.

Maybe I was dying and my life was flashing before me – but why would I remember a particularly bad comic-book at a time like this?

Or maybe I was dreaming – having a nightmare, actually, and that would be more likely to make me remember the worst comic-books I had ever read.

Or the comic-book publishers – Zargexon Comics – had made a film of "Earth Invaders" number 72 and that's what I was about to see.

Or – and this was increasingly starting to look like the most probable explanation – I really was captured and tied to a table by aliens who looked revolting.

"Dad?" I whispered again. "This would be a really good time for you to wake up!"

No reply. I hoped he was OK, wherever he was.

But for now, I was on my own and had to look after myself.

But, looking on the bright side – and there was one, despite the fact that I was a prisoner of ugly aliens – I had all of dad's super-powers!

Which was a dream come true!

After all, why did I read comic-books anyway?

I suppose it was because I wanted to be a super-hero myself, to have amazing powers and fight horrible enemies!

And now I could!

Hurray!

It wasn't easy to clear my mind from all the thoughts that were going through it, but the outcome of my inner struggle to do so was that while anyone else would have been terrified by this situation, I was loving it!

It was great to feel so powerful!

But – focus, focus, focus.

I just have to find out what's going on and remain alive long enough for my dad to wake up and take over again, and then we could all go home.

Until then, I had to stay here.

Wherever here was.

Presumably I was within that same complex of underground caves and tunnels we'd just been exploring. And I could scan around with my - or my dad's! - super-vision to pin down my location, but I was rather pre-occupied with this extremely ugly alien.

I suppose in another situation I would be scared of it, but in this one, I wasn't.

I just found it extremely ugly.

Still, it probably thought the same thing about me.

I looked at the horrible thing for a few more minutes, expecting it to speak, but it didn't. Maybe it couldn't. So it was up to me.

"Hello?" I said, and waited for a response.

The tentacles carried on waving, the eyes were blinking – at different times from each other – and the mouth opened and closed, but no sound came out of it in reply.

"Hello?" I said again. "Is there anybody there?" I waited again, and was rewarded with a reply.

"Earthborn," it said, in a deep, growling voice, "do you understand me?"

It was hard to connect the sounds with the movements of the mouth, but it seemed as though the creature was talking to me. Also, there was a small tube going into the mouth from somewhere off-screen. Maybe it was to feed the alien, or possibly to help it to breathe. Either way it didn't help to make its speech any clearer.

"Yep," I replied. "I sure do. Do you understand me?"

Several of the eyes blinked at the same time. I hoped that meant something good.

"I do. Your language is knowing to us."

"Oh good," I replied. I should have been scared, I suppose, but in fact I was curious. And pleased that we had made contact at last. "Why have you captured me? What do you want?"

The mouth moved randomly, and more sounds came out of it.

"We will take over all the earthborns."

"Oh," I said. "That's all right, then."

No surprises there for the experienced comics fan. After all, that's what aliens usually wanted. Except for the Pogungneds, of course, in Universe Team's opening issue. They'd wanted to become professional footballers and win the World Cup. Still, there's no accounting for taste.

Especially amongst aliens.

Chapter 13

Language Lessons

I even felt a little bit disappointed. This was such a cliché. I mean, if it had said, "we plan to turn the Earth into a giant marshmallow and feed it to the cosmic snail of Quimbox," I would have been really interested.

Or even, "we will kidnap all of your soap actors and turn them into exploding supernovas." Well, at least they would have become stars in their own right.

But no.

It was the usual "take over the human race" bit.

Had this creature read no comic-books at all?

Didn't it know we'd heard it all a thousand times before?

Presumably not.

I sighed.

And gave the chains a slight tug.

It was almost enough to snap them.

So I didn't feel trapped, because I knew I could escape at any time.

Until then I decided to keep this creature talking, and find out more about it before I revealed my true strength.

"Hmm, how do you intend to do that, then?" I asked. Maybe this creature liked to chat.

"I'm glad you asking," growled the creature in reply. "I like to chat."

Right I was. Probably it liked to practice its English. Dad once had a Spanish friend, Pedro, who used to come and stay with us sometimes, and he always said he liked to practice his English. He did slowly get better, it was true, so maybe the practice worked. It might work for the alien, too.

The creature spoke once more. "I like to practice my English."

Ah. Right I was again.

Still, it seemed a bit ironic. Here was I, bursting with super-powers, and an alien had captured me so it could use me for language lessons.

That was a storyline you didn't come across too often in the world of comics. Not even in the bad ones. I mean, it didn't exactly have an epic ring to it, did it?

Think of Galaxo, arch enemy of Q-Force. He used to swallow entire universes for breakfast. Now that was epic. That was terror on a cosmic scale.

But this world-conquering alien of mine?

He wanted English lessons.

Ah well.

Dad's Spanish friend was really grateful. Maybe the alien would be too.

It was my turn to say something.

"That's nice," I said. And then, just to keep the conversation going, I asked, "and what's your name?" I would have been so happy if he'd said 'Pedro.' I thought the name kind of suited him.

"Before I telling you," growled Pedro - well, I'm going to call him that anyway - "I must asking you a question."

"Go ahead," I replied. "I'm not going anywhere." In my mind I added the word "yet," but he wasn't to know that. I noticed that dad still wasn't awake, but I put my anxiety on hold.

There would be time for that later.

If dad didn't come back.

But I couldn't afford to think like that.

"Why is it that you are still awaking?" Pedro asked.

I thought about this. I didn't know the answer, but thought it wise not to tell him that. In the comics they always kept the baddie talking until he said something they could exploit.

"Well, that's a good question," I replied, stalling for time. "It's obvious, isn't it?"

It wasn't at all obvious to me, but I had to try and trick the alien somehow.

"Is it obvious?" Pedro growled. "Not to me. Every human has always falling to our weapon. You are the first one to be not."

Interesting.

They'd chained me up, but it didn't look as though they were aware of my super-powers, although that may have had something to do with why I hadn't been affected.

I had to keep Pedro talking until I found something out. Then I could break free and….and do something else. I didn't know what, yet.

"Well, maybe your weapon's broken," I replied, nonchalantly.

"No, I thinking not. It has working very well lately. How my English is, by the way?"

"Very good," I replied casually. "But surely you must get the chance to practice on those humans I saw on the assembly line. You could chat with them anytime, couldn't you?"

"Alas, no," Pedro replied. Then it said, "Is that being good English? It seems old-fashioned to me."

"Yeah, to me too. I'd cut that out of your vocabulary if I were you."

"But you not me. And never will be, so why saying it?"

My dad's Spanish friend, the real Pedro, used to make comments like that, too. It was really annoying.

"It's just something we say. It's not important. And anyway, why did you say 'alas, no'? Why don't you practice your English on those other people? They are your prisoners, aren't they? So they can't escape when you want to chat to them in English, can they?"

"It is being true that they our prisoners and can't escaping," growled Pedro, "but you see, the weapon worked on them, the one that didn't working on you."

"So what is this weapon supposed to do?" I asked.

"It destroying human minds and turning humans into slaves. Brainslaves we calling them. Except for you. Which is strange."

I was glad to hear this. I was quite fond of my mind and definitely didn't want it destroyed.

"Oh well," I said, casually. "It must be broken, then. Or it needs a new battery. Shouldn't you take it back to the shop? Or is it out of warranty?"

I was ready to break my chains, but I still felt I didn't know enough. I needed to find out more.

"So how am I different from the others, then?" I asked.

"You are not, as far as I can telling, although I may have to performing a dissection to be sure. You seem to being a fully-grown human adult, just like all the other brainslaves."

I noticed something this time. A key word. "Adult?" I repeated. "Your weapon is designed to be used on adults?"

"Of course," replied Pedro. His deep voice became

louder, as if he was annoyed. "Why would we wanting any younger-than-adults? They have no strength. They are too rebelling. They do not comply easily. We only taking human adults for brainslaves, not younger ones."

I got it.

I got it at last.

They had a weapon that destroyed people's minds.

But only the minds of adults.

Not children.

Not teenagers.

Only adults.

Which meant that I was still awake, conscious and in control inside dad's head because I wasn't an adult.

But dad is.

Or was.

Where is he?

What had their weapon done to him....

I began to feel the anger rising up from deep down.

Just like the incredible Hunk.

It was like a volcano building up pressure inside me.

Dad!

My dad!

They had taken his mind away with their weapon, leaving my mind alone in his head.

That was why I had total possession! That was why I wasn't just a passenger any more!

He wasn't here!

They'd taken him!

Taken him away!

But where to?

I was on the edge of bursting my chains, but there

was just one more thing I needed to know.

"So what happens to the adult minds?" I asked, pretending to be unconcerned. It probably wouldn't be a good idea to give away how urgently I wanted to know the answer to this question. "You know, the ones you brainslave."

I was flexing my muscles. The anger was proving hard to contain.

"The weapon storing them. We may needing them for another use one day. Sometimes they are useful to put into warrior. It depending, as I think you saying in English. Am I right?"

The anger had turned into a rushing sound in my ears, and now I knew I'd heard enough. I had to find this weapon and release my dad – and presumably all of the other brainslaves, too.

My anger blossomed.

I roared.

Like a lion.

And snapped all of my restraining chains like strips of paper.

I sat up on the table and peeled the metal bands off my wrists and ankles as easily as unwrapping a candy. Then I leaped off the table and looked up at the alien on the screen.

"This is what a human being can do," I said, wagging a finger at him sternly. "And now – I'm coming for you!"

"No, you mustn't, you don't understanding…" the creature began, his growl beginning to waver.

"I understand well enough," I replied, and smacked my hand on the metal table I'd been tied to. It split in half, and fell in pieces onto the floor. "And now it's time you understood something, too."

I'd never felt so angry, and so determined to make a point.

"You do not..." I began, looking straight at the screen. I picked up a metal table leg from the floor and bent it in half. "You absolutely do not..." I went on, folding the metal leg into a pretzel shape. "You really, really, really do not..." I continued, taking the knotted metal and squeezing it into a tiny ball, "...really do not want to mess with the human race."

I hurled the tiny metal sphere at the screen with the alien's face still on it. The expression was unreadable, but that didn't matter because it wasn't there for much longer. The screen smashed into a thousand tiny pieces as the metal ball hit it.

I blew the metal dust off my hands. I had broken and folded and compressed a piece of metal, and I wasn't even breathing heavily. It was easy peasy. Because I was so incredibly strong.

"And now," I spoke out loud, not caring whether I could be heard or not, "my little bug-eyed monster, I'm coming to find you, ready or not!"

I smashed open the metal door and stepped into the corridor outside.

Chapter 14
Letting Rip

I knew I had to move quickly.

I didn't know what those aliens might do to me or to the brainslaved prisoners.

Or to their stored minds.

So I had to find that hairy creature as soon as possible and force it to release my dad and everyone else who'd been caught.

And give them their minds back.

So I walked down the corridor while scanning through all the walls with dad's super-vision thingy, to discover exactly where I was going and also to find out where the alien who'd been speaking to me was.

I didn't know if there was only one of them or many, so I had to work on the basis that there were many just in case there were.

I scanned and I scanned with dad's super-vision, but I'd never imagined how hard it would be to actually use it. I finally understood what dad had meant about it being difficult. It always looked so easy in the comic-books, but actually using super-vision was like, well, like focusing a telescope or binoculars or a camera. It required continual concentration to find and maintain a clear image, and even more of it to understand what I was seeing, so it wasn't as easy as I'd thought.

Which is why, when I finally found the alien – and, as it turned out, all the other aliens too – I was confused by what I thought I'd discovered. I knew my control of super-vision wasn't perfect, so I wasn't very confident about the quality of what I thought I was seeing.

But anyway, at least I'd located them! They were a few rooms away, and there were quite a lot of them in there. They all had that weird face, and their bodies weren't much different from it either, but I decided to get to them as quickly as possible.

So I didn't try to work out which route would take me to where they were. I just bashed my way straight through the intervening rooms and corridors. Walls, machines, technical equipment, I cut my way through them all with my bare hands.

Super-strength was a great thing to have. As was a tough skin. Was I bullet-proof too? I don't know. All I do know is that it didn't hurt my hands at all to chop though metal.

I moved fast.

Very fast.

Super fast.

Thank heaven dad had got super-speed!

I was too fast for those creatures, who must have been following my progress on some kind of CCTV. And who would hopefully be terrified of me by the time I got to them.

And then suddenly, I was there!

I burst into their room, prepared for an all-out fight.

A tussle.

A wrestle.

A battle of the titans.

Me, against a squad of huge, hairy, tentacled aliens.

But I didn't need to worry.

I told you, didn't I, that my mastery of dad's super-vision wasn't brilliant yet?

That it was hard to control and interpret?

Which was why I'd made the mistake.

I'd got their size wrong.

I was in such a hurry that I hadn't studied them properly.

Or sensibly.

Or else I would have realized the truth.

And the truth was…

These aliens were not very big.

Not very big at all, actually.

In height they only came up to my knees.

So, quite small aliens, in fact.

Just because the screen was big, I'd assumed that Pedro was big, too.

But he wasn't. Whichever one he was.

He was tiny. They were all tiny.

I was flummoxed.

It was like walking into a room of stuffed toys.

Or over-sized puppets.

Ones which moved all by themselves.

And which wore backpacks with tubes attached, tubes that went all the way to their mouths.

All of which combined to make them look, well, not at all threatening.

"Uh, hi guys," I said as I looked down at them.

"Hi, earthborn," they squeaked back in reply.

Their voices were really quite – well, squeaky. Pedro had had a deep, growling voice, but it must have been modified by the speaker or the microphone he'd been talking through so as to impress me.

And to scare me.

Well, I wasn't scared any more.

Because they weren't at all threatening.

Until they shot me, that is.

Or, should I say, shot at me.

Several beams of something hot struck me, but I felt no pain. They burned my clothes, leaving black spots, but I didn't feel a thing. I smiled as they continued to shoot at me.

"Now then, kids," I began. They were the size of very small children, so I didn't feel I could call them anything else. "Just calm down, before I lose my temper and do something we'll all regret."

Those peculiar round mouths in the middle of their faces all hung open. It was time to press the advantage of my shock-and-awe entrance, and show them what I really could do. If only I knew myself!

But I had a good idea what to start with.

Super-speed.

I knew exactly which ones had shot me. They were holding small metal zapping rods in their tentacles.

Did I mention they didn't have hands? Or feet? Or arms? Or legs?

Just tentacles, technically.

Quite a lot of them.

Not like an octopus, with eight thick ones, but lots and lots of little ones, in constant motion. Oh, and as well as that they all had tubes in their mouths, attached to small packs on their backs.

And some of these cuddly little aliens were holding the zapping things they'd been zapping me with.

So it seemed like a good idea to confiscate them – at super-speed.

In the blink of an eye – or of many eyes, in their case – I had run round this clump of aliens and taken away their weapons.

With super-strength I squeezed them all together and crushed them into powder, which I brushed off my hands onto the floor. "Anything else?" I asked. I was feeling pretty confident that I could handle whatever they might throw at me.

"Yes," squeaked a tiny voice, and all of the little creatures ran over to one side of the room just as a door on the other side opened. Through it ran one of the big green monsters we'd seen caged up. With a scream it launched itself at me, reaching for my throat with its sharp talons.

Now let's face it, I should have been terrified at this point. I mean, the thing was at least twice my size – which is to say, twice my dad's size as I was in his body – and bulging with muscles. It was almost as big as the incredible Hunk, and twice as scary.

However, I had total faith in my new-found powers.

With super-speed I nipped under his claws, and with super-strength I punched him right on the chest.

What a crunch! Several ribs must have broken!

And, to my surprise – and utter delight! – the big green thing flew backwards through the door he'd come in by, at about ten times the speed. There was a distant crashing sound as he hit something very solid.

And my hand wasn't even the tiniest bit sore.

I turned to the knee-high aliens.

"Anything else?" I asked.

Before they could reply I decided to impress them. With my left hand I sent a wave of freezing cold which in only a few seconds had them all frozen solid and covered with icicles. Before it could hurt them too much I sent a burst of heat from my right hand, and thawed them out so that the melted icicles left small puddles on the floor.

The aliens staggered with the sudden shock of being released from their frozen state, but before they could recover I delivered my final surprise. I raised both hands above my head and sent a blast of lightning through the ceiling.

It made a hole big enough for me to fly through should I need to make a quick escape, and the roof of the cave was clearly visible through it.

Don't ask me how I knew how to do all these things. I just did!

It was amazing!

I was amazing!

I blew the tips of my fingers one by one, just like a cowboy blowing the barrel of a smoking gun after firing a particularly impressive shot.

"I said – anything else? Or was no-one listening?"

I was enjoying this.

I was born to be a super-hero, and by golly, I really was one at last! I adopted the classic super-hero pose - you know, hands on hips, chest puffed out - and looked down on the aliens with a scowl.

The little creatures were gathered together in a huddle, tentacles overlapping, and they were humming intensely in a slightly annoying way.

"Well?" I asked at last. "I haven't got all day!" I was getting restless and was quite prepared to put more pressure on the aliens. I was tougher than them, after all.

Then they stopped humming and all turned to face me.

I prepared myself for another attack, another blast, another assault, and was ready to respond with over-

-whelming force.

I was quite looking forward to it, actually, which was why I was pretty disappointed with what actually did happen.

They threw themselves on their faces in front of me, and grovelled.

Chapter 15

The Reason Why

"Uh, guys? Guys? You can get up now," I said.

I was glad they weren't attacking me any more, but this was a surprising outcome. I mean, it looked as though they were surrendering.

To me!

How cool was that?

Edison, saviour of the world!

"Uh, guys? You can get up now! Please?" It was a bit embarrassing to have a bunch of aliens grovelling in terror on the floor in front of me, plus it was going to be a bit boring if they were so frightened of me they wouldn't even talk.

One of the tentacled creatures got up from the floor. I wasn't sure, but he sort of looked familiar. Maybe it was something to do with the pattern of the eyes on his face.

"Uh, was it you that was speaking to me on the screen? You know, when I was tied down?"

"That is right, earthborn. Or shall I calling you sir? I believe that is correcting in English for a higher status male?"

"Uh, yeah, sir is fine." No-one had ever called me sir before, least of all an alien called Pedro. Well, called Pedro by me, that is. While we were talking, the other aliens stood up too.

"Very good, sir. I'm sorry we are trying to hurt you, but we are having scared."

"Yes, OK, I can understand that, but I haven't done anything to scare you, have I? I haven't threatened you at all, yet you're attacking me. That's not right, is it?"

"It is what we must doing. We must defending the project. It is life and death for us and our whole civilization."

For the first time I had something to hold onto. "What exactly is your project?" I asked keenly.

"You, sirs, are the harming of our expedition. The people of ours are depending on us completely. For the rescue of our civilization. You see. Possibly helping us could you with your mighty power, sir."

All of the creatures bowed to me, touching their faces to the floor. Still, they didn't have far to go. Their tentacles were so short.

"Hang on, hang on, hang on. Are you asking *me* to do *you* a favour? *Me*, who you captured and attacked with guns and a green monster? *You*, who've got monsters chained up and have brain-dead humans working as slaves?" I couldn't believe their cheek! "You must be mad! I think I'm going to smash this place up and release all of your prisoners, monsters or no monsters!"

"No, no, dear sirs, please, you must not be the doing of this. Our peoples are depend on us!"

All of the little wriggly things started squirming and moaning, as though they could all understand our conversation. If that was true I wanted another view, another opinion.

"Hey, someone else say something. Is Pedro the only one here who can speak English? Or can another one of you back him up?"

"To being sure, sir, I can," said a different voice, but still with that high-pitched squeaky quality. "He be speaking is true. We are making protection here for our own people back at home. If stopping us, you will kill all. Every one!"

There was no doubt they were doing bad things to us humans, but they did seem to have some sort of reason for doing it. I was certainly going to stop them, but I needed to know what they were doing and why, not least of all so I could get my dad back.

I picked up a table, folded it in half, squashed it into a cube, put it on the floor and sat on it. "Well," I said, relishing the power that I had, "why don't you explain everything to me before I get bored and start smashing the whole place up? And let me warn you…" - I was wagging a finger at them at this point - "I'm not very patient. My temper is short, and it's building up. So you'd better be quick with the explanations."

I crossed my legs and looked at them.

They were humming again.

Eventually, one of them was pushed forward by the others.

"You seeing, sir, we need warriors. Soldiers. Those to fighting. We come from a planet where there being two races. Us – we are Kragellyans, from Kragellya – who are peaceful and calm and nice and gentle and tranquil and helpful and…"

"Yes, yes, I get the idea," I interrupted, "you're the good guys in this conflict."

"Yes sirs, we are being the very good people. But there is a bad people who hating us. They hating us to death and tries all to kill. They are the evil Vorbraxa. We are fighting them for many long cycles of your time and ours also."

"So you've come here to escape from these – these evil Vorbrax thingies, have you? You want to take over our planet and leave yours behind, do you? Well, I'm not having that! This is our planet, and ours alone! You can't have it!"

"No, no, sirs, this not being our task! You see, we are small – even on our planet – so we do not be good at the fighting. That is why we have coming here to make an army and taking it back with us! We are recruiting a defence force! It is an army we are the building and collecting here, an army to taking home and fighting for Kragellya!"

"Oh," I said.

This did ring a bell.

It wasn't the first time I'd come across this idea. The Invigilators faced an enemy who turned frogs into dinosaurs to help them fight an opponent of theirs back in the Negative Zone. And there were similar storylines in Amazing Fantastic Spectacularly Awesome Comics back in the 1950s.

So these little things - these Kragellyans - were here to recruit humans to be warriors for them, to fight against an aggressive predator back home - the Vorbraxa. But they weren't giving the humans a choice! They were kidnapping them! I'd made my decision.

"Look, little guys, you can't just steal our people, you know. I mean, you didn't even ask them if they wanted to assemble spaceships or be turned into monsters, did you?"

"We didn't wanting the ask because they not be agreeing. Surely."

"That's right. But you could have advertised, you know! There are always some people who like to fight. Retired soldiers, off-duty policemen, unemployed mercenaries. I bet you could easily have raised an army if you'd been willing to pay for it!"

"This is not understanding. Everyones must always be forced to do what we wanting to do."

"OK, so diplomacy's not your strongest point. But still, you can't just kidnap humans to use like pets or toys or slaves! Can't you find someone or something else on a different planet? Go and enslave another race in another star system and leave us alone!"

I was running out of patience. I'd given them a chance to explain themselves, but I wasn't getting anywhere.

I stood up.

"Anyway, that's enough chat. I need you to release your prisoners before I smash up this place and send you home. Go and find another planet to pick on!"

I put my hands on my hips in the classic super-hero pose again, and tried to look intimidating.

Well, I don't know how I looked, but I felt pretty awesome. All that energy pulsing through me made me feel good, I can tell you, and I was bursting with a new-found confidence that I could sort out these weird little creatures.

"Well?" I said. "What are you waiting for? Release the prisoners and start packing up! Now! Do it before I lose my temper! Grrrrrr!" I growled at them just to reinforce my point.

The little things hummed again, rushed around and bumped into each other, and then another one was pushed out of the bunch to talk to me.

"Being sorry, sirs, but there is nowhere else. Near us. Near enough. That is."

"What do you mean, there's nowhere else? Just find

yourself another planet. Any one will do, but not this one. Go and harass someone else."

"I trying to explain, sirs, but is no-one else. You and us are alone. On this side of the galaxy, anyway."

I stood for a moment in silence. We were alone? Only two inhabited planets? They must be joking, surely. It went against every tradition of comics writing that I'd ever come across.

"What are you saying? There are millions of worlds out there, aren't there?"

"Yes sirs, many worlds, but not many living possible. Not many at all. Only two we know of. Ours and yours. So the Vorbraxa are always trying to steal our land – there is so little habitable living space in the universe…"

I had to think again.

I couldn't believe this.

My science teacher had said there were billions of stars and so lots and lots of planets…

Maybe these aliens were trying to trick me. Unfortunately, I couldn't decide if they were or they weren't. I had no way of telling the difference. Probably it was all an excuse anyway. Well, I couldn't afford to be sidetracked. "I don't care, really," I said, trying not to think about it. "Just return the brainslaves to normal."

They started humming again.

I was getting frustrated. They were delaying all the time. "What is it now?"

I showed my teeth and snarled. They jumped and hummed once more. I liked scaring them. No-one had ever been scared of me before.

Still, I was actually in dad's body and I did have his

super-powers. They had good reason to be scared of me!

"So what's the problem?" I demanded. "Release the prisoners you've zombified, and turn the monsters back into humans. And I want it done now!"

"Sirs, everything not is so easy. We cannot be unmaking the whole army in a second."

"Well, how long will it take, then?" Classic superhero pose. Hands on hips. Radiate superiority.

"It taking many of your cycles."

"Cycles? You mean years?"

"Years, yes, sirs. It has taking us many years to make them, so it will taking many years to unmake them."

"I think you'd better explain yourselves!"

"But first, sirs, may I asking you a question?"

I had the feeling that this was just a delaying tactic, that they were wasting time and beating around the bush. But my dad was waiting to be released, and I couldn't wait any longer to do it!

"OK, then. But hurry up and ask!"

I was approaching the end of my tether.

Soon I would have to start punching something!

Chapter 16
A Hero is Born

"Sirs, we are having a questioning. You are powerful very, it is clear. More than many warriors in one."

I think that was a sort of complement, but I wasn't quite sure.

"We have not finding humans like you before," squeaked the alien, "humans of great power. What are you?"

I pulled myself up to dad's full height, puffed out his chest and looked down on them in as arrogant a manner as I possibly could. I tried to project overwhelming self-confidence, but I wasn't quite sure how to as I'd never done it before. I gave it a go anyway.

"You know nothing about the protectors of humanity, do you? You see, I am not just human. I am super-human. I am..." I struggled to give myself a name or description. This was the moment when the super-hero announces himself to the world and I had to do it properly! "...I am – **SUPER-HERO DAD**! Nothing can conquer me!" And just to get them really scared – because I didn't actually know how powerful they were, and I needed to make the greatest possible impression on them – I added, "and I am only one of many of my kind. We police the planet Earth, and protect it from all dangers. So far you have escaped our notice, but now that I have found you I will alert all my colleagues the world over, and the, uh, Army of Super-Hero Dads will destroy you and all of your works. Unless you leave immediately, of course!"

It was all a bluff, obviously, but it sounded good to

me. I smiled confidently at them and puffed my chest out even more. Dad didn't have a very big chest, and I don't know if it made much of an impressive spectacle when it was puffed out, but it seemed to me to be the right thing to do in any case.

Then I had an inspiration. I don't know why I suddenly remembered it just then, but it came to me in a flash. Right back at the beginning, when I'd first tested dad for his powers, he'd lifted me off the ground with telekinesis. I'd forgotten about it until now, but this was just the right moment to use it. Not that I knew how to, of course, but hey, that wasn't going to stop me from trying!

I looked at the group of aliens standing in front of me, and I imagined them all rising up into the air in a clump. Guess what? That's exactly what they did! They wriggled and squeaked as they did so, but nothing could stop me from lifting them up to the ceiling, and holding them there for a minute.

Then I switched on dad's glow and rapidly cranked it up to maximum. It was dazzling! Even I couldn't see properly! But what I could see was that the aliens had stopped wriggling and were basically paralysed with fear! "Good outcome," I thought, and gave myself an imaginary pat on the back. Then I switched off the glow and dropped them onto the floor. This obviously made them squeak quite loudly, and I left them collapsed on the floor for a few more minutes until I delivered my ultimatum.

"OK, little squirmy people," I said, in the most intimidating way I could. It felt strange to use my dad's voice. I mean, mine wasn't a deep one at all, and while I didn't think of my dad as having a deep voice either, his was certainly deeper than mine!

Anyway, I made it as deep as I could.

And put on as fierce a face as I could muster.

"Your time is up. The first thing you're going to do is reverse the brainslave beam and give all your slaves their minds back. Then you're going to un-mutate those poor monsters and let all the people go. And if you don't feel like doing any of those things, not only will I smash up this whole place and destroy every piece of equipment in sight, but I will wreck all your space-ships and make absolutely sure that you never get back to your home planet ever again. Or would you prefer that I **_KILL_** you all instead?"

I shouted the last part.

I wanted to scare them into submission.

Because I certainly couldn't carry out my threat.

I couldn't even kill a fly.

But they weren't to know that.

The little things were jumping up and down and running round in circles, bumping into each other.

"Well?" I asked. "Release your prisoners or never go home again. Decide – **_NOW!_**"

I stamped the floor, and it cracked. Nice effect, I thought. But I had to be careful with this super-strength. I really didn't want to break anything. Well, not yet anyway. Not until dad was released.

The creatures had squashed themselves into a huddle. Their humming was so intense that they seemed to me to be arguing among themselves.

"I'm waiting," I said. "I'm going to count down from five, and then I'm going to start breaking things up, starting with your space-ships. I think you'll find it a long walk home!" I had to keep the pressure up. I couldn't give them even a second to think of a new plan against me. I didn't know what other fancy and dangerous items of alien technology they might have up their sleeves – not that they had any sleeves. "Five, four, three…"

One of the small tentacled creatures burst out of the huddle and ran towards me.

"No, no, sirs," it cried. "We will do it. We will releasing the prisoners. Do not break up our ships. We would rather return home than be stucking here!"

I nodded my head wisely. Mind you, I don't know if head nodding meant anything at all to an alien that didn't have a head it could nod. It only had a body with a face on the top bit of it. "Good decision. You can start with the brainslaves. Release them all."

Three of the creatures ran to a bunch of lights and buttons and switches on the wall and started pressing and switching things with their tentacles. I hoped and prayed that this was going to bring dad back. What would I do if it didn't?

I had to trust that they were obeying my orders. The only influence I had over them was fear. So I growled and stamped my foot once again. The cracks in the floor spread out further.

It had the desired effect, though. The aliens started to work even faster.

After a few more seconds they stopped and turned to me. "It is done," one of them said.

"Dad?" I whispered inside my head, while maintaining my fierce exterior to the aliens. I was scared and lonely in here. What if it didn't work?

What if dad didn't come back?

"Dad?" I whispered a bit more urgently. "Are you

there?"

I waited nervously for a few more seconds.

And then I heard it.

Dad's voice.

"Eddie?" he said, sounding drowsy, as though he'd just woken up. "Eddie? Is that you? I've been asleep, I think, but now I'm awake again."

Dad was back!

Chapter 17

Undoing the Evil

"Dad! I can't believe it! I'm so glad you're here!" I couldn't help myself blurting it out.

"Here? Have I been somewhere? And where are we – and what on Earth are those?"

"It's a long story, dad."

I couldn't know for sure the aliens were really telling the truth or not when they said that the brainslave beam removed people's minds and stored them, rather than destroying them. I only had their word for it, and I wasn't inclined to trust that very much! But it seemed that they were telling the truth after all, thank goodness!

It looked as though I was lucky.

And dad was too!

And then I noticed.

I wasn't in control any more.

I couldn't feel my hands and feet.

I mean, *his* hands and feet.

Now dad's mind was back, he'd automatically taken control of his body again.

And put me in the back seat once more.

Ah, well.

I'd enjoyed having super-powers.

And being an adult.

But I suppose this body did belong to its rightful owner.

Dad.

Whew, it was so good to have him back again!

I would've given him a hug if I hadn't been inside his head!

But how was I to explain what had happened while he was away?

"Uh, dad, while you were…asleep…I kind of took over and found these aliens." They were looking at us apprehensively. They didn't know we were having this secret conversation inside our head. "They're responsible for all the kidnapping that's been going on lately…"

And so I told him the whole story.

As well as I understood it.

And as well as you do, too.

But you see, my dad's clever.

He's got an engineer's brain. You know, one that works properly. Not like mine. And he grasped everything immediately. I was so happy just to sit back and let him take over - and make all the difficult decisions!

He finished listening to me and turned his attention to the aliens. He knew just what to say next.

"So, are all the brainslaves released now?" he demanded. He wasn't going to let on that we had our own private way of knowing whether they'd been released or not!

"Yes sir, Super-hero dad, sir."

I felt him look at me inwardly. I hadn't told him about his new name.

"Prove it!" he insisted, in his firmest voice. I hadn't quite managed to sound as strict as him. I guess it took practice to get the most out of a voice.

"Yes sir, Super-hero dad, sir," they replied.

Screens lit up on the walls all over the room, and we could see what was happening in the caves outside. The humans who'd been unloading the trains and assembling the space-ships had all stopped the work they were doing, and were looking around themselves in a puzzled and confused sort of way.

"I think I'd better go and help them, son," dad said to me privately. Then, aloud, he said to the aliens, "I'm going to go and help those people and take them home. While I'm away don't try anything funny or I'll know about it. In this time you can work out how to un-mutate the monsters. I'll be back to help with that too, so don't you dare hurt them or try to escape."

I could feel dad's anger from the inside, and the little aliens were shaking as he spoke to them. They looked scared, as far as I could tell! I didn't think they would try a double cross, but you never can be sure.

I poked dad with an idea. He took it up immediately and spoke firmly to the aliens.

"I can and will check on you at any time, because I can see through solid matter even from miles away. I will be keeping an eye on you wherever I am, and I will be back."

The aliens stood completely still, and then slowly bowed. I think they got the message.

Well, the next part of the story was a bit dull, but necessary. I'll tell it to you quickly. Dad used his super-vision to find all the possible ways out of the aliens' underground complex. He didn't want the rescued brainslaves all appearing in the basement of his factory, so he had to find another way of returning them to the outside world.

He found it.

The aliens clearly had several ways of getting in and out of their cave complex to kidnap people, some of whom were kidnapped from quite far away.

A network of tunnels led to the outside world on both sides of the mountains. Dad used his super-vision to find the easiest way out which led away from our own town, and which deposited the people within walking distance of another one.

It wouldn't have been kind to dump them in the middle of nowhere!

Dad got all the people onto a train and persuaded one of them to drive it for him. All kinds of people had been kidnapped, and luckily amongst them was a train driver!

The people were all so confused that there was little chance of any of them finding their way back into the caves. And, of course, they had no idea what they'd been doing all the time they'd been brainslaved.

I couldn't wait to see tomorrow's newspapers and the TV news reports. The coverage of all the returning kidnapped people was bound to be amazing, even if none of them could remember anything about their kidnapping!

The rescued people got out of the train in some kind of secret railway parking place. It was in a hollow in the mountainside, and once the people had all left the train and were climbing up the embankment to the road which would take them to the city, dad pushed the train back into the tunnel – there was no-one left to drive it – and closed the tunnel exit by punching the inside wall until the rocky ceiling collapsed. It was a useful thing to have super-strength!

Then we flew down the tunnel back to the main network of caves, and returned to the control room. It was time to solve the problem of the monsters!

While we were flying I had the chance to look over the whole complex of cages.

There were rows and rows of growling beasts. It looked as though there were several hundred of them. The Kragellyans must have been kidnapping the residents of Barnchester and the nearby towns for years. I knew that people had been disappearing for a long time – it was always in the news – but I didn't know for how long. I hadn't given it that much attention really. I was usually focused on my comic-books, after all! Maybe the Kragellyans had already shipped some of the mutated people back to Kragellya (or whatever it was called) – maybe they'd already been killed in the Vorbraxa wars!

It was up to us to stop this and return all the monsters to their real human lives again.

I could feel dad's tension rising inside him.

"Dad?" I said.

"Yes, Ed?" he replied.

"What are we going to do about the monsters?"

"Well, we have to get them back to being human again, obviously. At all costs, Ed, at all costs. How would you like to be trapped in a body like that, and sent to an alien world to fight some other kind of monster? No, Ed, we owe it to them to return them to normal. And I'm going to make sure those aliens do it."

Now my dad was a pretty easy-going kind of dude.

It took a lot to get him angry.

But now he was getting really angry.

And with power like his, he could get an awful lot

done with that anger!

And I think he was going to do just that.

With his super-vision he scanned the whole control complex. There were a few Kragellyans scattered around the place, operating machines, but most of them were in the control room where we'd left them before.

At least, I suppose it was the control room. Anyway, it was where they were all huddled.

The Kragellyans turned to meet us as we arrived back through the hole in the ceiling. They began humming again.

"You know what I'm going to say, don't you?" he said to them. They bowed down and then up a few times. I suppose that was as close to nodding as they could get without a neck.

"I want the monsters returned to human shape. Now."

There was a humming and a scuffling as the Kragellyans changed positions in their scrum.

"Sir, Super-hero dad, sir, we have never doing this before. It has not never been doing before, sir, ever."

"Then you'd better learn how to do it. Fast. Or I will be launching you into space, one at a time. Without a ship."

We stared at them pretty hard, I can tell you. I was really proud of dad, standing firm like that. But hey, let's face it, he was right. We had to get everybody back to normal. Imagine if dad was one of those monsters, or mum. How would I feel? How would they feel? We had to help those poor people return to normal. And dad was in no mood for messing about, I can tell you.

"Why don't you start by telling me how they got that way? We can work backwards from there." He's a clever man, my dad.

The aliens all hummed in a huddle again. At last they spoke. Well, one of them did. ""Very well, Superhero dad, sir. We have two kinds of warriors. You have seen, yes?"

"Yes, of course. Green and brown. Is that the only difference?"

"No sirs. You see, at home the Vorbraxa have two environments, wet and dry. Tropical forest and arid desert. So the green ones being for the wet forest environment. We making those by mutating the humans chemically. They are bathing in a powerful liquid, quite slimy and sticky." A screen showed an image of some glowing green gooey bubbling liquid, pouring into a vat from a tube. I had an idea. "Dad? Is that what I think it is?"

"You bet it is, son. That's what I fell into last night. They must make it in our factory and pipe it out here underground. I don't think I was meant to fall into it, though. I think that part was an accident. Someone must have been doing some maintenance and just left the cover off the drain hole."

The little Kragellyan continued. "The mutations produced are very strong, and their skin becomes hard. Sometimes they also glow."

"That's you, dad. Or at least, one bit of you!"

"Yes, son, that is part of the explanation of what happened to me." Then he spoke out loud to the Kragellyan. "And what about the others? The desert warriors?"

"Yes sir. They are mutated with a special beam of ours. We sometimes using the same beam to capture people from your cities. It pulls them up into our ship while mutating them."

Things were really beginning to fall into place now! "Dad! That was the other thing! The alien ship that zapped you! It was trying to capture you and turn you into a desert warrior!"

"Right again, son. Lucky the ship and I were struck by lightning – that stopped the kidnap and the mutation!"

"Did it, though? I wonder what the mutation is? Ask him."

"So, little alien, what is this beam meant to do? What is the mutation it creates in the people it zaps?"

"In the desert they must attack the enemy swiftly and with cunning. There is nowhere to hide on the flat desert land, so attacks must be rapid and well co-ordinated."

I had a bad feeling I knew what was coming next.

"So what fighting qualities does the mutation beam give them?" dad insisted again.

"They can fly, they are telepathic, and their senses are enhanced," replied the tentacle creature.

"Meaning what?" dad asked weakly. He'd guessed it too.

"Meaning they can see far away. Very far away."

I was nearly jumping up and down inside dad's head.

"It's you again, dad! You've got those powers as well!"

"Yeah," he said, reluctantly. "I'm a kind of blend of those two monsters. That's not very nice, is it?"

"No, if you put it like that, I suppose not. But you're more than that. You're better than that. You've got their best aspects without their – well, without their ugliness, I suppose."

"Yeah, that's true. I should be grateful for that, shouldn't I?"

"You bet!"

"But why aren't I ugly like the monsters? Like *both* monsters?"

"Well dad, speaking as an expert on super-powers, aliens, monsters and mutations, I would like to refer you to "Protease Pete," number 271, when the legendary Pete turned two alien cultures that were attacking him against each other, thus wiping them both out. I know this isn't exactly the same thing, but what if the two mutating agents – the chemical goo and the zapping beam – cancel out the worst part of each other's mutating effects, which is to say, the horrible appearance?"

"But then shouldn't their powers be cancelled out as well?"

"Ah, but the lightning blasted you *after* you'd been zapped by the ray from the space-ship, and that fixed the powers that it gave you, so that when you fell into the chemical goo the powers *that* gave you were added to the ray-zapping powers instead of cancelling them out, so…"

"You're making this up, Eddie," interrupted dad, in a confused sort of way.

"No, I'm not actually. It's quite similar to a storyline in "Captain Cosmos," where the Captain…but you don't need to know all that. Why not just try getting the aliens to treat each kind of mutation with the opposite mutating agent? It didn't work for you because you'd been blasted by lightning in-between the two treatments, but for them it should mean that the two mutations cancel each other out."

"Don't you think this could be dangerous for them? It might make things worse!"

"How could they be worse off than they already are? They can't exactly go home looking the way they do now, can they?"

"No, but the alternative is that they might end up being twice as monstrous, and then they would be really hard to control."

"Good point. I hadn't thought of that. Well, Captain Cosmos did it, so it's worth a try."

"That's good enough for me. It wouldn't have been before yesterday, but now I'm prepared to believe anything."

"Tell them, then."

"I will." Dad cleared his throat with an anticipatory cough. "I've decided what to do," he said out loud. "You are going to cure the warriors by treating them with the opposite mutating agent. Tropical with desert, and desert with tropical. That will return them to normal. And you'd better make sure that it does."

The aliens went crazy. They hummed a lot, and ran round bumping into each other. After a few minutes of this they threw themselves at dad's feet again.

At our feet, I mean.

This was becoming a bit of a habit.

"Come on, kids," said dad. I can understand him calling them kids. They were very small, chaotic, emotional and unruly. The fact that they were capable of doing destructive things to thousands of people didn't really seem to enter into it. "Come on now. I'm starting to get annoyed, and you really don't want that to happen, not when you consider what I can do!"

I think he was enjoying his power!

"Please stop grovelling! What's the problem now?"

A voice came out of the crowd.

"How did sirs knowing? How could he be guessing? The answer you have. We would never being tell you that, but we must honouring the truth. You have succeeding in guess the secret. It is true. The opposites cancel out."

I mentally high-fived dad inside his head. "Well done, son," he whispered. "I really must read more comic-books."

"No need to, dad, when you've got a specialist like me on board!"

"Good kid." Then he spoke out loud again. "Then do it, and don't waste any more time! These people have been trapped in mutated bodies for long enough! Get to it before I smash this place up!"

Chapter 18
A Parting Gift

I don't need to tell you about the rest. First of all dad made me go back into my own head at home and explain to mum what he was doing and why. That was because we didn't know how long all this would take, and so we might arrive home late in the evening. Or in the middle of the night. Who could say?

Then I came back again and joined him as he forced the aliens to do as he wanted. It turned out they knew perfectly well that the mutations could be reversed this way. In fact, that's exactly what they were planning to do once they'd won their war and didn't need the warriors any more. They'd return them to their human state, and then keep them as brainslaves. They were much more useful for technical tasks as humans than they were as monsters.

So the aliens prepared the vats of goo for the desert types, and the zapping beams for the tropical types, and hey presto, they all turned back into human beings again! Then they had to be de-brainslaved as well, so they all got their minds back. Of course, we had to find clothes for them, lots of them, but the aliens had a stash of those too, meant for the assembly workers who'd now gone. They really had been catering for an entire army!

Dad repeated his trick of delivering them to the outside world by train, but took a different route this time. He left them, confused and memory-free, beside a motorway service-station on the other side of the mountains. Which left nothing to resolve, except for the aliens themselves!

Dad and I flew back along the abandoned tunnels.

I felt good. We felt good.

We'd released thousands of people, who could now return to their normal lives.

The disappearance blight had been ended. All the missing adults had been returned to the outside world.

Now all that remained was to do something with the aliens.

Those small, tentacled, cuddly little things.

Which weren't really cuddly little things at all!

The huge cavern was strangely quiet as we returned to it.

No more monsters squeaking, growling or howling.

No more machinery rumbling and beeping.

No more trains arriving and no more space-ships being assembled.

Nothing but peace and quiet.

"It's time for those little fellers to go home now," said dad.

"Yep," I replied. "I hope they have a working space-ship to take them back."

"Oh yes, they have a few. I'll disable the ones they leave behind so they can't use them in the future."

Just as he spoke we flew through the hole in the roof of the control room once more.

The Kragellyans were sitting disconsolately on the floor.

Or lying down.

It was hard to tell which.

"So, dear little aliens, it's time for you to go home. I've returned all your prisoners to the outside world, so you've got to go back to yours."

Several of the creatures moaned. They sounded ill.

Or depressed.

"Come on," said dad. "What is it now? Out with it."

One of the Kragellyans spoke up at last. I thought it might be Pedro, but I wasn't quite sure. "Oh, Superhero dad, sir, we have doing all you said because we fearing you. But we fearing even more what will happen to us if we going home without army. You do not know our generals. They will surely killing us all."

Personally, I felt they deserved it. I mean, they had ruined the lives of thousands of human beings just for their own selfish reasons. I thought they were due for some kind of serious punishment.

Dad wasn't like me, though. He was kinder.

"Look, guys, why not take some other wildlife from Earth? Something you could take lots and lots of, and no-one would mind, something you could mutate to your heart's content? Something which is pretty unpleasant to begin with, so it would probably turn out to be a fearsome warrior when you've mutated it?"

The little creatures were picking themselves up from the floor. One of them spoke. "Do you knowing of a species like this? We find Earth creatures too many and varied for us to studying. That's why we focusing on the dominant species."

"I know just the thing for you. You'll have to do some serious mutation on it, but I think you'll find it makes an excellent warrior. Wait here. I'll be back."

Dad flew up out of the hole in the ceiling again, and flew down the tunnel we'd originally entered the cavern by, the one that led back to his factory.

The one where the train had nearly squashed us against the roof.

There were no trains now, of course, so the flight

was an easy one.

And very, very fast.

Wow, when dad let rip, he really could fly! And I think he enjoyed it, too.

I certainly did!

"Where are we going, dad?"

"You'll see, son, and I'm sure you'll understand."

In no time at all we'd climbed through the hole in the wall dad had punched when he came out of the lift. Then he pressed the button to call the lift down, and in a few minutes we got out of it, several levels higher up.

We were in dad's staff canteen. It was open twenty-four hours a day because those were the hours the factory was open.

Now remember that dad's clothes had been burned by laser guns when the aliens attacked me, so he wasn't exactly looking smart.

But neither was anyone else here for that matter (because lots of people were wearing greasy factory clothes), so a few burn-holes didn't attract any attention at all.

"Hi Harry," said a couple of guys as dad strode past them.

"Pete, Bill," he nodded in reply.

No-one bothered him. It was his normal work canteen after all. Why shouldn't he be there? But then he did something out of the ordinary. He didn't queue up to collect some food. Instead, he went straight into the kitchen.

A number of heads turned round. The cooks, who were cooking. They weren't used to seeing him there, that was for sure, from the looks on their faces.

"Uh, hi guys. Uh, do you have one of those plastic boxes to put sandwiches in?"

One of them nodded.

"You do? Thanks."

Dad spoke in such an authoritative way that no-one questioned him. One of the assistants took a big, lidded plastic box out of a cupboard and handed it to him.

I loved the way they all looked at us. It was surprised and...respectful. Dad's personality had changed from what it used to be before the accidents. Now he radiated confidence, and everyone who met him could feel it.

"Cool," dad said as he took the box. "Thanks again," and we carried on walking into one of the store-rooms. The cooks didn't pay us any more attention at all, as though we had every right to be there. Super-hero dad rules!

"Dad!" I hissed. "What are you looking for?"

"Watch," he said, and he switched on his super-vision and shared it with me. We were in a room which was full of stacks of shelves, shelves which were packed with loaves of bread, together with rolls and biscuits too. There were crumbs everywhere, all over the place.

He scanned the walls and focused his vision on what was just beneath the surface, inside the wall itself.

And there we saw lots of little tunnels.

With lots of cockroaches in them.

"Yuk!" I said in disgust. "You're not going to, are you?"

"You bet I am!" he said, and he strode right up to

the wall, located a big nest of the horrible insects, punched his hand through the plaster and the bricks and started to fill the big box with the wriggling creatures.

Now, he undoubtedly had super-speed, super-strength and a super-tough skin, so it would be no problem at all for him to scoop a couple of hundred unwilling cockroaches into a plastic box in just a few seconds. But in fact, what happened was that the cockroaches all piled into the box by themselves! When he closed the lid on the full box, others were still queuing patiently to get into it! "Sorry guys," dad said. "Maybe next time." The cockroaches disappeared in a flash, as though they'd been dismissed by a boss.

A master.

A king?

"Dad?" I whispered in amazement. "What did you just do there?"

"Let's talk about it another time, son," he said. "We're in a kind of hurry now, aren't we?"

I was left wondering what else he was capable of as we retraced our steps to the underground tunnel.

Only a matter of minutes later we were back in the cave with the Kragellyans. Dad was handing over the box packed tight with wriggling cockroaches to one of the little aliens who were standing in the doorway of a space-ship.

"What is this thing, Super-hero dad, sir?" the little creature asked.

"This is the beginning of your new warrior army," he replied. "Here on Earth we call these things cockroaches. They can live anywhere, eat anything, survive harsh conditions, and multiply rapidly. If you play around with their genes and mutate them you will get the warriors you want. If anything, they could even prove too dangerous for you to handle, but that's your problem."

He then put on a very stern voice, as if talking to a bunch of small children. "And if you ever return to Earth I will deal with you harshly, very harshly indeed. You have no idea how lucky you are. Now off you go, and don't you ***EVER*** come back!!!"

"Do not have the worrying, Super-hero dad, sir, we will return to Zargexon and stay there. Earth is no longer safe for us." The space-ship door began to slide shut.

"Dad?" I said.

"DAD?" I shouted.

"What is it, son?"

"What did he say the name of his planet is?"

Dad called to the creatures just as the door was closing. "Didn't you say you are Kragellyans?" he called out. "Isn't your planet called Kragell, or something like that?"

"Super-hero dad, sirs, for a powerful being your memory is not very good. Our continent is called Kragellya. Our enemies live on the continent of Vorbraxa. Together we live on the planet of Zargexon."

Another one piped up, "Come and visiting us sometimes, sirs, if you please. We will giving you a tour." It might have been Pedro, but I couldn't really be sure.

Then the door closed. The space-ship rose up into the air and the roof of the cave slid open. The space-

-ship disappeared into the opening in the roof, and we never saw it again. I suppose it flew out of the top of the mountain.

So they were from a planet called Zargexon?

What a coincidence that there should be a comic-book publisher called Zargexon Comics!

Chapter 19
The Newest Issue

Dad flew around the cavern system. It was huge. There were tunnels and side-tunnels, sub-caves and super-caves. There were areas for manufacture, assembly and storage. And, of course, there was a fleet of space-ships, all ready to take the warriors back to Zargexon. We made sure that every single door, exit, air vent, any and every way in from the outside world, was closed, sealed, blocked. Kaput.

Sometimes dad forced in pieces of metal to jam sliding doors. Other times he pulled down the tunnel ceilings, to fill them with fallen rocks. He was thorough, was my dad.

He didn't destroy anything inside the complex – the trains, the tools, the equipment, the offices, even the space-ships. He left them all intact.

"Dad? Are you going to leave it all in working condition? I mean, they might come back, mightn't they? Isn't it dangerous to leave everything here so they could use it again? Especially the mutation equipment and the space-ships!"

"You're right son, but the engineer in me doesn't like to break up working machines. I've sealed everything thoroughly. No-one and nothing can get in, not even a cockroach, let alone the aliens! I've sealed their escape route in the roof, too, remember, so they can't come back in that way either."

"OK then. So what's next?"

"Well, this may seem hard to believe, son, but it's late at night, and we've been here since early this morning. I expect mum will be worried. And I'll get into trouble with my boss for disappearing from my work all day."

"Yeah, but you did save the world, didn't you?"

"True, but I can't tell him that, can I?"

And with that, dad turned off the power supply to the cave complex and switched on his glow. It was the only light left in that subterranean world, and he kept it on until we'd flown to the end of the long train tunnel for the last time. Then he fixed the wall he'd broken in the basement to get into the tunnel, and we went back up the lift to his office.

Everyone had gone home. He just had to grab his coat and leave too, so that's what we did.

The next morning I had a long lie-in. At least, I meant to, but I actually woke up quite early. So much had happened the day before that I just couldn't go back to sleep. Every second of every moment went round and round inside my head.

Especially the time when I had control of dad's body.

And I had super-powers.

Me.

Myself.

A super-hero!

I could remember the tingle, the buzz, the pulsating energy of having unlimited power, and the sheer confidence that came with it. I remembered the moment when the aliens had zapped me with their laser guns or whatever they were, and I'd felt nothing.

Nothing at all!

My clothes had burned, but there weren't any marks on my body. Dad's body, that is. It had been amazing. Wonderful. If only I could have…

And then it hit me. The very last thing the aliens had said. That they were from the planet Zargexon. Now it could just be a coincidence, but did this have anything to do with…Zargexon Comics?

Surely not.

So against my better principles and years of devoted laziness, I got out of bed. I knew where to look. Underneath my bed, in the Comics Dungeon, where all the worst comic-books lived.

The ones with the worst artwork. Or storylines. Or both.

Interestingly enough, Zargexon Comics usually fell into both categories.

But the main reason was the artwork. I mean, the drawing was always a bit, well, wobbly. It was as though we were looking at the pictures through water, or hot air, or some kind of gas fumes. Sort of unfocused.

And the stories were always – and I mean always – about aliens from other planets fighting each other across the galaxy and trying to take over the Earth. It got boring after a while.

But…

There was too much of a coincidence here.

I had to find out more.

I had to speak to someone at Zargexon Comics, someone who could tell me what they knew about the Kragellyans and the Vorbraxa. I had to find an address, or at least a phone number.

So I pulled out 'Earth Invaders' numbers 1 to 25,

and looked inside the front cover of every single one of them to discover the place where you'd expect to find the publisher's contact details. But there was nothing there. Not in any of them. I checked out the whole series, right up to the latest issue, number 93. No publisher's address.

Then I looked through 'Attack from the Stars.' It was the same.

And 'Underground Slaves.' And 'Kriozoc, World-Eater.' And 'Servants of Groaloz.'

Every single issue.

No address, no phone number, no website, no email.

There was only one thing to do.

Enlist specialist aid.

So I hurriedly got dressed, threw down some breakfast, made my excuses and headed out for the main meeting place in town for comic-book addicts.

The Nineteenth Dimension.

Well, you've probably realized by now that today is Sunday, so what's the point of going to the comic-book store on a Sunday?

And the answer is that comic-book addicts need their fix 24/7. And, as most of us are still at school, Saturday and Sunday are our best days for hanging out together and discussing the latest comic-book gossip, such as; did Floorman really kill the Golden Zodiac for the third time, or was it just a dream?

You know the kind of stuff.

But today I had other things on my mind. I needed to know the contact details of Zargexon Comics. I had to speak to someone there to find out what they knew about – well, about you know what.

I pushed through the usual Sunday crowd outside Nineteenth Dimension, and stepped into paradise.

For me, anyway. And for hordes of comic-book fans too.

On the walls – all over the walls, from floor to ceiling – were shelves and shelves of the latest issues.

And on the floor – from wall to wall – were bins and bins of back issues and vintage comics.

Collector's items were locked in glass cases, selling for prices people like me could only dream about. I mean, issue number one of "Terrible Zombie Dancers" from 1973, was selling for £850!

If I had it, I'd pay it.

I hadn't had more than a couple of seconds to absorb the intoxicating vibes created by a million comic-books crammed into a small shop when Dave grabbed hold of me. He was the owner. He lived and breathed comics. What he didn't know about them wasn't worth knowing. Although his name was Dave, we all knew him as the King. Because he was the King of Comics. Well, in our small world, anyway.

"Hey, King," I said urgently, "what can you tell me about…"

I was about to say "Zargexon Comics," when he interrupted me.

"Hey, Eddie boy," he said, holding up a brand new shiny edition of something I hadn't seen before. "I know you collect this weird stuff. You're the only one of my regulars who does. This one came in just this morning, so I've kept it for you. Not that it's likely to sell, but I know you like this rubbish. Here. Have a look. I didn't even know it was in the pipeline. It could be a one-off, or the beginning of a series, I dunno which. Anyway, take a look at it."

I took the magazine from the King's hand, and my jaw dropped. I know they say things like that a lot in comics and books, but mine really did. Drop, that is. My mouth fell open so wide that any passing fly would have had trouble avoiding it. My eyes popped out of my head, too.

Well, not completely, but almost.

The comic-book.

Was.

Called.

Wait for it.

'SUPER-HERO DAD.'

On the cover was a drawing of what was probably my dad, but it was hard to tell with that blurry, watery style of drawing, like a camera out of focus…which meant that this must be a Zargexon Comics publication!

I opened it so fast I nearly ripped the cover off.

Sure enough, on the inside page it said, "Zargexon Comics Publications," but there was no address!

Dave had to know the answer to this.

"Hey, King," I said, raising my eyes from the unexpected magazine.

"Yes, pal?" he replied. "Do you like it? Want to buy it? The artwork isn't so good, but that's Zargexon for you. I don't know how they stay in business. No-one buys them except you."

"Yeah, sure, King, I'll take it. Uh, you don't happen to know where their HQ is, do you? There's never any address in the mag."

"Why do you want to know that?"

"Well, uh, I want to write to their letters page. You know, saying how much I like it and that kind of stuff."

I was bluffing, of course, but what else could I say?

"There isn't a letters page in there," said the King, in his deadpan way. "I looked."

"Yeah, well, they might start one if I write in, mightn't they?" I argued. I wasn't going to let up on this one. I had to find out more. I had to.

"Sorry, pal. I don't deal with Zargexon direct. I just get them in from the distributor. You could try them. They're called..." he looked in a box of index cards "...Speedy Literature. They handle all the publishers. Here," he added, and he wrote their phone number down on a piece of paper for me. "Give them a ring."

"Thanks, pal," I said, as I took the number. "I'll do that."

I handed him the money for "Super-Hero Dad," and left the shop in a bad mood.

I gave the dudes a nod as I walked through the crowd, holding the rolled-up comic-book tightly in my hand. I didn't want them to see what I was carrying! I didn't want anyone to know about it until I'd read it, anyway. I strolled with pretended nonchalance to the end of the road, and then, when I'd turned the corner, I ran.

I ran as fast as I could to the park.

And there I sat on a bench in the Sunday morning sunshine and read the latest publication from Zargexon Comics.

I couldn't believe my eyes!

It told the story of yesterday. The story of how the

aliens came to Earth to create two types of warriors by mutating human beings. How they kidnapped people to do it.

And how my dad arrived, with super-powers, and sent the aliens on their way.

I nearly fell off the park bench.

For someone to know all this, they must have been there yesterday.

Watching.

Spying.

On the aliens.

And on us!

But luckily, there was no mention of me sharing dad's head. They didn't know about that, obviously.

But everything else was there.

Even up to the aliens flying away with the cockroaches, and dad sealing all the exits, and then flying away down a long tunnel.

So someone - a someone who makes Zargexon Comics - was there watching everything. Or, alternatively, had cameras planted there, and was watching it remotely.

I'd reached the next-to-last page of the story. Dad had just flown away, and there was one page left to go. What could be on it?

I turned over to find out.

There was a picture of an office, with people sitting at desks, drawing and writing. And talking to each other. They all looked a bit Japanese. As it was a Zargexon Comic, and everything was slightly out of focus, it was hard to be sure. Anyway, in a series of panels, the conversation went something like this.

"Hey guys, aren't you sad that this is our last

issue?"

"Not really. It's time we all went home anyway."

"But what if someone wants to send us a 'Good Luck' card, to wish us well on our journey?"

"Well then, they can write to 'Zargexon Comics, Groaloz House, Volex Street, Hogby, VP3 4AZ.' We'd love to get some messages."

"Especially from Super-Hero Dad."

"Yeah. Especially as this is our last comic-book ever."

"Yeah. Bye folks. Thanks for reading."

The last panel of the last page of the story showed all the staff in the office waving to the reader and calling out, "Bye bye."

I jumped up from the park bench and sprinted home.

I knew where dad and I were going today.

No, not today.

Now.

This minute.

Hogby.

Wherever that was.

Chapter 20

Going Home

It's cold up in the air.

Which is why dad had told me to dress warmly.

Because we were flying to Hogby.

We weren't going by plane, and I wasn't inside his head.

I was sitting in his back while he flew above the clouds.

I hadn't sat on my dad's back since I was about five years old, and he was pretending to be my horse.

Now he was my aeroplane, and he wasn't pretending.

We were both wearing swimming goggles to protect our eyes, and headphones to keep our ears warm. And we were wrapped up in woolly jumpers, coats, gloves and bobble hats, because, let me tell you, it is REALLY cold above the clouds.

Dad was steering with his super-sight-vision-thingy. He'd memorized the route from a road atlas, and was following the M97 motorway, which he could see through the clouds below us. We maintained telepathic contact, but I wasn't sharing his eyes and ears. I wanted to be present at Zargexon Comics myself, so I could ask them questions.

I was, after all, a comics expert.

"Are we nearly there, dad?" I asked him for the thousandth time.

I had to do it telepathically, as we couldn't hear anything with our headphones on.

"Well, finally I can announce that the answer to that

question is – yes, we are nearly there. Hogby is just below us, and I'm looking for a landing place now."

Dad started spiralling down through the clouds. I was beginning to feel a bit dizzy when he let out a whoop. "Well, well, well, they've made it easier for us!" he cried. "Look at this!"

He sent me the image of the town below that he could see with his super-sight. It was a big industrial city with factories and office blocks, but then he zoomed-in his super-vision thingy onto the flat roof of the tallest office building in the city centre beneath us. It was easy to spot because the whole top of the building was coloured green, and had words painted on it in huge yellow capital letters. They spelled out the words, 'ZARGEXON COMICS WELCOMES SUPER-HERO DAD!'

"Uh, I think we've found them, dad."

"Yep. Or, to be more precise, they've found us."

"Well, you mean they're expecting us, don't you?"

"I do. And I'm pretty sure that comic-book was intended to bring us here too."

"Yeah. For sure. Let's go and see what they want, shall we?"

"Do you think it's a trap?"

"Dunno. I really have no idea. Hang on, though. You don't think it could be those Kragellyans trying to have their revenge on us, do you?"

"Could be. I'll have a look inside."

I was still sharing dad's vision – while holding tight onto the back of his coat so I didn't fall off – as he looked inside the building.

There were a few floors of offices on the top of it, and underneath them were printing presses and huge rolling machinery of the kind needed to produce newspapers and magazines, or, in this case, comic-books.

"Hey, dad, that's kinda cool. They write them, draw them and print them all in the same building."

"I suppose you'd call that total control."

"Yeah. Obsessive, actually. Still, that's the only way they could've turned out your comic-book so quickly."

"True."

I'd started calling the "Super-Hero Dad" issue I'd bought at Nineteenth Dimension 'your comic-book' as soon as I'd shown it to him..

I liked his new name, but I'm not sure he did.

I think he was a bit embarrassed.

Plus, I don't think he'd realized yet that it was me who'd given him that name, when the brainslave beam had zapped him and I was in control of his body. Which was something he never asked me about. Maybe he didn't even remember having a blank spot in his memory.

The Sunday newspapers had been full of the news of the returning disappeared, and absolutely none of those who'd gone back to their previous lives could say where they'd been all the time they'd been missing. They had no memory of that time at all. Not even a recollection of dad leading them to safety. It seems their memories only really began once they were in the outside world again. For them there was no gap in their memory from the moment they were kidnapped by the aliens to the moment they returned to normality. No blank spot at all.

Maybe it was the same for dad.

Hopefully it was.

I pulled myself out of his head and back into my own as we approached the flat roof of the Zargexon Comics building. We kept the telepathic link, though, just in case.

I slid off his back as we landed. I must say his control was pretty good for someone who'd only learned to fly the day before.

It took a few seconds for me to find my balance on a solid surface again, and I think it was the same for dad. We'd been flying for about two hours, and we'd both totally adjusted to it.

Also, here it was warm. Compared to above the clouds, that is.

So we took off our coats, gloves, hats, woolly jumpers, goggles and headphones and left them in a neat pile in the corner of the flat roof, just beside the very large yellow 'Z' of 'ZARGEXON.'

There was a door. A fire escape exit. And it was open.

"This should be interesting," said dad.

I nodded.

I was much too nervous to speak. We approached the door and dad went in first. There was a staircase going down, and that's where we went.

After about a minute, there was another door.

"What's behind it, dad?" I whispered, this time with my real voice in his real ear.

"An office," he replied. "*The* office. The same as in the comic-book. Exactly the same. With the same people."

"Oh," I said. Well, at least we'd come to the right place. "Let's go in, then. I expect they're expecting us."

Dad nodded his agreement, and then opened the door.

We stepped into the room.

Every head turned to face us.

And look at us.

There was a moment of silence.

And then everyone was cheering. And clapping. And rushing towards us.

It was amazing!

In only a few seconds we were surrounded by all the people who worked in the office, and they carried on clapping and cheering as they shook our hands and patted us on the back.

This was such a surprise that it took me a couple of seconds to realize that it was hard to see everything clearly in the office. It was a bit like looking through water. Or hot air. Or through an out-of-focus camera. In fact, it was just like reading a Zargexon Comic! And the people looked – well, they looked slightly Japanese.

I rubbed my eyes.

It made no difference.

Suddenly, a voice cut through the cheerful noise. It was slightly strange - a bit metallic and with a hint of a Japanese accent, but quite friendly and extremely enthusiastic.

"Friends! Dear friends! Let us welcome our hero! Our saviour – and his companion. Please, come in, Super-Hero Dad, and be welcome among us!"

I wasn't surprised to hear the greeting. It was obvious. They'd wanted us to come, after all, hadn't they? But I don't think dad quite expected it. He was a clever man and a brilliant engineer (I think), but he was a bit short on imagination.

"How – how do you know me? And why do you call me that?"

"Come in! Come in and we will tell you all. Please, sit down. And I think this must be your son, yes? He looks like you. He is a comic-book fan, I think, yes?"

I nodded. I'd expected nothing other than this. It felt so cool to know exactly what was going on when my dad didn't have a clue.

Dad and I sat down in the middle of the office, and all the staff gathered around us. Dad rubbed his eyes a bit. I expect he was having trouble focusing too. The one who'd welcomed us seemed to be in charge.

"Who are you?" dad asked him, suspiciously, "and why have you called us here?"

"My dear, dear sir, my name is Deralatos, and I am the leader of our colony here. We are so, so happy to welcome you to our dwelling, and you must understand that there is nothing bad in our intent. You see, we wanted to thank you before we go home."

"Before you go home? Thank me? But why? What's this all about?" Dad was getting ever so slightly annoyed. If I didn't calm him down this could lead to some kind of disaster, and there was no need for that, no need at all.

"Dad, it's OK. They're friendly. I think I can explain everything. Well, most of it, anyway."

You see, when I went home with the 'Super-Hero Dad' issue, I gave it to him to read. I knew that would keep him occupied for a while, as would researching the route we would need to take to get to Hogby.

So I used that time well.

I dug out all my Zargexon Comics publications, and flicked through every single one of them.

I'd read them all at some time before in the past, of course, but I'd forgotten the story-lines.

Now I was reminding myself. And as I re-read them, I saw them in a different light. I read them not as fantastic stories, but as history. As fact. As telling us something that really had happened. And so I looked through the 'Planet of Doom' series, the 'Earth Invaders' series, the 'Servants of Groaloz' epic, and, of course, 'Kriozoc, World-Eater.' And all the others, too.

It had taken me a little while, but by the time dad was ready to go, I'd sorted out the explanation for everything.

I'd never felt so useful in all my life.

It was time for me to speak up.

"So, hi guys, you don't know me, but my name's Eddie, and I'm the son of, uh, Super-Hero Dad." Everyone smiled at me in their blurred and Japanese way. Some nodded, some waved, and some said, "Hi Eddie."

"I'm a big fan of comic-books. A regular collector, you might say." There were more smiles and nods of approval. "And I've got every issue of every magazine you've ever produced." More nods and smiles. "And I think I've worked out your story from reading them." Even more nods and smiles. These people really were in a good mood. Something to do with going home, I suppose.

"Ed, you didn't tell me!" said dad, in a hurt tone.

"I've literally only just worked it out today, dad. Trust me. I know what I'm doing."

He nodded silently. I cleared my throat, and began my prepared speech.

"Zargexon Comics publications started printing just over five years ago. The first series, 'Kriozoc, World-Eater,' told how an ancient evil had arisen on a distant planet, and the population of that planet had split into two warring factions, one with and one against the legendary Kriozoc. 'Planet of Doom' told stories of battles between these two factions, and 'Warrior Monsters' and 'Agents of Andromeda' described wars taking place throughout the galaxy. 'Earth Invaders' brought the story to our own planet, and your other publications describe how the two groups struggled for supremacy across the universe.

"The common theme was that the evil faction took over friendly planets and turned their inhabitants into soldiers to fight on their side in the wars back on the home planet.

"The good faction followed them wherever they went, to carry the battle wherever it needed to go to stop the evil faction from sending more soldiers back to the home planet to fight against them."

I looked around.

The staff were smiling at me and gently nodding. I knew I was going in the right direction.

"The Kragellyans my dad defeated yesterday were the evil faction, the servants of Kriozoc, the World-Eater. You..." - I looked around the room once more - "...are their enemies, the servants of Groaloz the Wise. You are the Vorbraxa. And you have been writing and printing your comic-books here ever since you – and they – arrived on our planet, to warn us about what they were doing.

"And, as you would never kidnap or mutate humans to help you in your struggle, you preferred to tell your story to our world in the form of comic-books, so that someone here on Earth would recognize what the Kragellyans were doing and stop them. Am I right?"

"Very good, very good, young master, you are right," said Deralatos. The rest of them cheered and clapped. "And can you guess the rest?"

"I think I can," I replied confidently. "When they told us yesterday that you are the aggressor, they were lying, which is typical of the followers of Kriozoc. *They* are the bad guys, and you are the good guys. And you had their whole base wired with cameras so you could spy on them all the time, which is why you saw everything that happened yesterday.

"And because they've gone back, you want to go back too. But you wanted to thank my dad before you went, so you published an urgent and once-only issue of "Super-Hero Dad." You were hoping that someone would read it, recognize him and tell him about it – and I did, so here we are!"

"Very good, young master! And truly a grand master, I must say, which is what we must call those who carry our history for future generations! You were correct on every point! But there is one extra thing you have not mentioned, and I suspect by the look on his face that your father is about to say it. Yes, dear Super-Hero Dad, please do speak"

"Excuse me, I find all this hard to believe, but I suppose I have to, as I've become part of it. Eddie seems to know who you are, and I trust him, so I must trust you too.

"However, if I am to believe that you represent the

'good' faction in your own war at home on Zargexon, I think I've done you some harm. You see, I felt pity for the Kragellyans yesterday, as I'd deprived them of the soldiers they said they were relying on, so I gave them some cockroaches to mutate into warriors which they could use against – you! And your friends, I suppose. I'm sorry, but I didn't know any better. I meant to do them a favour because I pitied them, but it seems I chose the wrong side to support! Please forgive me, but I gave them something they could use as a weapon against you and your people!"

Deralatos slowly shook his head and spoke once more.

"My dear, dear, sir, I am grateful for your sentiments but you must not worry, you really must not worry! You see, your son is correct. We lacked the means to stop the Kragellyan's project here on this planet, so we published our material in the hope of inspiring someone on Earth to help us – and it worked! You helped us, and you drove them away! Now you may wonder why we are so jubilant when you say you have given them a weapon against us, but, my dear, dear sir, I must tell you that we have already been out to the supermarkets and shops and bought as much and as many of every kind of insecticide that we can find here on Earth! Our scientists will analyze it and create the most effective cockroach poison the universe has ever seen! So my dear sir, you have sent them on their way with an utterly useless weapon! Are you surprised that we are happy? That we can go home knowing they bring us no harm from this world, and also that they will never dare come back here because of you! My dear Super-Hero Dad, you are a hero to us and to our population!

"We, the Vorbraxa people of Zargexon, will never forget you, and your name and your deeds will forever be enshrined in the Chamber of Honour of our nation!"

It was dad's turn to drop his jaw onto his chest. He'd never expected anything like this! And neither had I, to be honest.

Although the comic-book geek inside me still had some questions.

"Uh, so what are your plans now? I mean, if your enemy has gone, are you still going to stay here?"

"No, no, my dear expert in matters historical," said Deralatos, "we must be on our way. The Kragellyans left yesterday, so we must be proceeding behind them as quickly as possible so we may start work on the cockroach poison as soon as may be. We want them to expend valuable resources developing what they think is a new weapon, and then, when they deploy their mutated cockroaches we will – pssst! – kill them all at a stroke! So we must be ready! We must be going today! In fact, right now, because we have spoken to you and we have no need to remain, so if you don't mind…"

I couldn't bear it. There was something else I just had to understand. "Wait, please, wait," I burst out. "There are a few things I need to know first."

"Yes, of course, grand master of our nation's history, what may I explain?"

"Well, first of all, what do you really look like? I mean, you resemble Japanese people, Japanese humans, but that can't be your real appearance.

"Secondly, why does all the artwork in your comic--books have a watery, unfocused feeling, like the atmosphere in this room? I find it hard to focus on you here, just as I find it hard to focus on the drawings in your comic-books. Can you explain this?

"And thirdly, is it true that Zargexon and Earth are the only planets capable of bearing life, because that's what the Kragellyans told me?"

The smiley leader of the Vorbraxa nodded wisely as he considered Eddie's requests. Finally, he spoke.

"The grand master of our nation's history asks us very good questions. He is truly a worthy son of Super-Hero Dad. I will pass you to Vahatros, our chief scientist." He indicated another more-or-less identical Japanese-looking office worker.

"Thank you, master," said Vahatros, who came close to me and bowed. "The Kragellyans work in secret and do not like to be seen. They also lack the ability or the technology to change their shape, so they can never mimic life on the worlds they invade. This is why they must always hide, and force other species to do their work for them.

"We, however, are more flexible. Our real shape may not be pleasant for you to look at, as it is something like what you would call a blob. We resemble your amoebae, but we are bigger, of course, and we can mould our form into any appearance we desire. So we have taken on this human shape in order to exist un-noticed in your world. We have learned that you call this particular shape Japanese, but we simply copied the first person we met on this planet. When our ship landed, we attached it to one of your buildings, and surprised a very nice man who was cleaning the stairs of the building below."

"The cleaner? The very first person you met was a

Japanese cleaner, so you copied him?"

"That is correct sir. And as for your second question – our own metabolism requires a greater degree of helium and nitrogen in the atmosphere than you are used to, although it is still safe for you to breathe for a short time. Here, in this office which is also our home on this planet, the atmosphere is adjusted to our needs – it has extra helium and nitrogen in it. This makes the air more refractive, and the transmission of light through it a little problematic, so I fear our artwork may have suffered because of this. I am sure that it has not affected our sales, though."

"No," I thought, "probably not. Everything about their comic-books is so bad that sales couldn't possibly get any worse. Still, now I understand their wobbly drawing – it's how they see the world in this thick atmosphere!"

Dad joined in the conversation inside my head. "And that's why the Kragellyans wore those breathing tubes. They couldn't change the atmosphere in their gigantic cave complex just to suit themselves." I nodded in agreement.

Vahatros started speaking again. "And as for your third question about the number of planets which are capable of bearing life – what the Kragellyans told you is a great lie. They spread this untruth wherever they travel. They think that dwellers of the planet they are invading will take pity on them if they say there is nowhere else for them to go, but nothing could be further from the truth. The universe is teeming with habitable worlds, enough for every species and life-form that will ever exist, without any of them ever having to fight each other for living room!"

"And so, my dear saviours," interrupted the leader, Deralatos, "I trust that your questions have been answered. We must begin our preparations to leave, so I'm afraid I must terminate this meeting, pleasant though it has been."

He held out his hand to dad, and he took it. "I'm glad we were able to help," he began, "and I hope…"

"Dad!" I interrupted, "look what you've done!"

Dad had forgotten his super-strength and had crushed the leader's hand to jelly. He didn't seem to mind, though. Dad released his hand, and it flapped. In fact, it began to dissolve, and the dissolution started spreading up his arm.

The other pseudo-Japanese staff members began to lose their shape too.

"Never mind, dear sirs," said the leader, "we are merely returning to our natural shape in preparation for take-off. Please, do not mind us at all. This way."

His head began to sag and lose its shape as he led us to the lift door.

"Now please, dear sirs, go straight down to the ground floor and step outside as soon as may be. That would please me greatly. And please, please wave to us as we depart. That is a human custom I adore." The lift doors opened and he pushed us inside. "Farewell, my dear sirs, and thank you."

"Goodbye," I called out, and dad said "Bye."

All of the people in the office seemed to be melting, like snowmen in the sunshine. The door closed completely, and the lift descended. It went right down to the ground floor without stopping, and when the door opened we stepped out of it and found ourselves standing on the street outside.

"That's strange," said dad, narrowly avoiding a collision with a pedestrian.

"Yeah," I agreed, almost walking into a lamp-post. "Now don't forget, he said to look up and wave." We crossed the street to stand on the pavement on the other side, and tipped our heads right back in order to look upwards and watch the top of the building, which was at least twenty storeys high.

"What are we supposed to see?" I said.

"Dunno," said dad. "Maybe they have a space-ship hidden on the roof. Or inside the lift shaft. I expect we'll see it go up pretty soon, as he was so keen to be off..."

"Yeah, but..."

What I was about to say next was lost in the explosive sound of a gigantic industrial roar.

"I think that's a jet engine," I shouted.

"Several, if you ask me," shouted dad in reply, and we continued to look up.

In a few seconds the space-ship showed itself. We were both wrong about its appearance. It wasn't anything like what we – and you – had expected!

As it lifted off in a cloud of flame and smoke, the Vorbraxa space-ship could clearly be seen as the top five floors of the building. They simply lifted up as a single cubic unit, with flames jetting downwards out of the bottom of it.

"So that's what they meant about the cleaner," said dad. "When they arrived they probably plopped their ship down on top of the building we just saw it leave, and when they explored they met the cleaner of the building below, who happened to be Japanese."

"I expect you're right. Wave, dad, wave to them. Remember, he asked us to."

Me and dad stood on the pavement and waved to the top part of the building, which was rapidly disappearing into the clouds. It was the second spaceship we'd seen off in two days, and we waved until it was no longer visible.

Then we looked at each other.

"So, what now?" I asked.

"Now we go home," dad replied.

No-one else on the street had noticed that a piece of one of the buildings had blasted off into space. It was really weird. Maybe that's why these aliens had chosen Hogby to live in. The people here didn't seem to notice things much.

"Hey, dad," I said.

"What?"

"No more Zargexon Comics."

"True. Oh well, that means you'll have nothing to complain about any more. But, look on the bright side. Your collection will become more valuable as time goes by, because they're not going to print any more of them."

"Yeah. That's true. Still, it'll be a long time before their value rises much above rock bottom."

"Speaking of which, do you have any money on you?" It was unusual for dad to ask me that. It was usually the other way round.

"A bit, yeah. Why?"

"Can I borrow it to help me pay for the train fare home? I didn't bring much with me."

"But aren't we going to fly?" I was gutted. I loved flying.

"Well, guess what we left on top of that building?"
"All our warm clothes?"
"Correct."
"Mum will be furious!"
"Correct."
"Oh well. I hope someone on Zargexon likes them."
"I don't suppose there's anyone there of the right size or shape to appreciate them."
"No, I suppose not."
"Shall we find the railway station, then?"
"Isn't that what super-sight is for?"
"I suppose so. This way."

And so me and dad wandered through the streets of Hogby, trying to find the railway station without getting ourselves run over. Flying was easier because there weren't any roads full of traffic in the sky.

We weren't in any hurry as we walked around the town, so we stopped in a café and had something to eat. Nobody sitting near us could possibly have guessed that we were talking about aliens from the planet Zargexon, and how we had stopped them from taking over the Earth.

It was just another Sunday afternoon for Super-Hero Dad – and son!

About the Author

As well as being a writer, Steve Moran is a musician, a storyteller, an actor, a puppeteer, and a scientist.

He used to collect comic-books when he was young, but sold his collection to start collecting coins instead. He's been regretting it ever since.

He lives with his wife, son and two cats in Sussex, England.

About the Author's Other Books

If you liked this book, you're sure to like Steve Moran's other books too! Why don't you try:

Jackie Potatoes
Starallax Revenger
Barnabus Mudpatch

A Children's Book of Cats

Suzie Sparkle and the Magic Book
Suzie Sparkle and the Dragon Princess
Suzie Sparkle and the Bewitched Picture

Printed in Great Britain
by Amazon